THE OFFICIAL GUIDE
TO THE VIRTUAL WORLD

Grosset & Dunlap
An Imprint of Penguin Group (USA) Inc.

LucasBooks

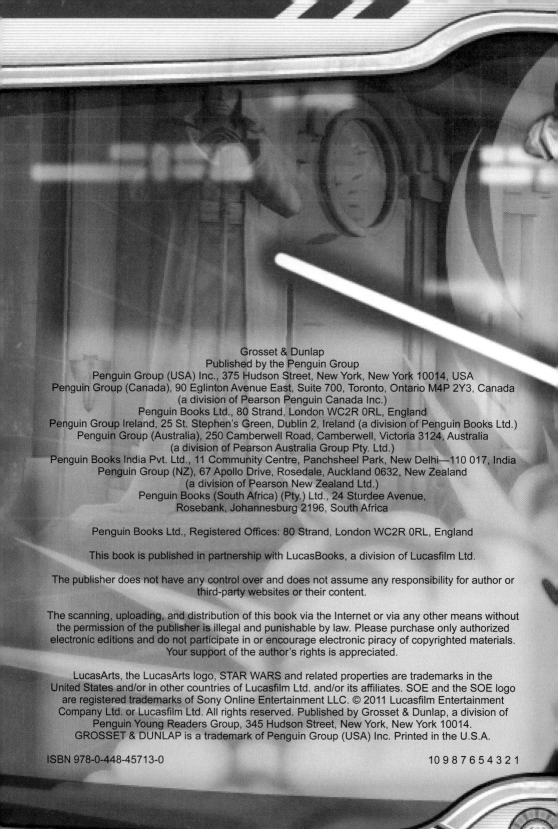

Grosset & Dunlap
Published by the Penguin Group
Penguin Group (USA) Inc., 375 Hudson Street, New York, New York 10014, USA
Penguin Group (Canada), 90 Eglinton Avenue East, Suite 700, Toronto, Ontario M4P 2Y3, Canada
(a division of Pearson Penguin Canada Inc.)
Penguin Books Ltd., 80 Strand, London WC2R 0RL, England
Penguin Group Ireland, 25 St. Stephen's Green, Dublin 2, Ireland (a division of Penguin Books Ltd.)
Penguin Group (Australia), 250 Camberwell Road, Camberwell, Victoria 3124, Australia
(a division of Pearson Australia Group Pty. Ltd.)
Penguin Books India Pvt. Ltd., 11 Community Centre, Panchsheel Park, New Delhi—110 017, India
Penguin Group (NZ), 67 Apollo Drive, Rosedale, Auckland 0632, New Zealand
(a division of Pearson New Zealand Ltd.)
Penguin Books (South Africa) (Pty.) Ltd., 24 Sturdee Avenue,
Rosebank, Johannesburg 2196, South Africa

Penguin Books Ltd., Registered Offices: 80 Strand, London WC2R 0RL, England

This book is published in partnership with LucasBooks, a division of Lucasfilm Ltd.

ISBN 978-0-448-45713-0   10 9 8 7 6 5 4 3 2 1

Contents

Part 3: Playing Games

Part 8: Making Friends

Part 9: Getting Help

To collect your exclusive
bonus code go to
www.penguin.com/clonewars
and follow the instructions.

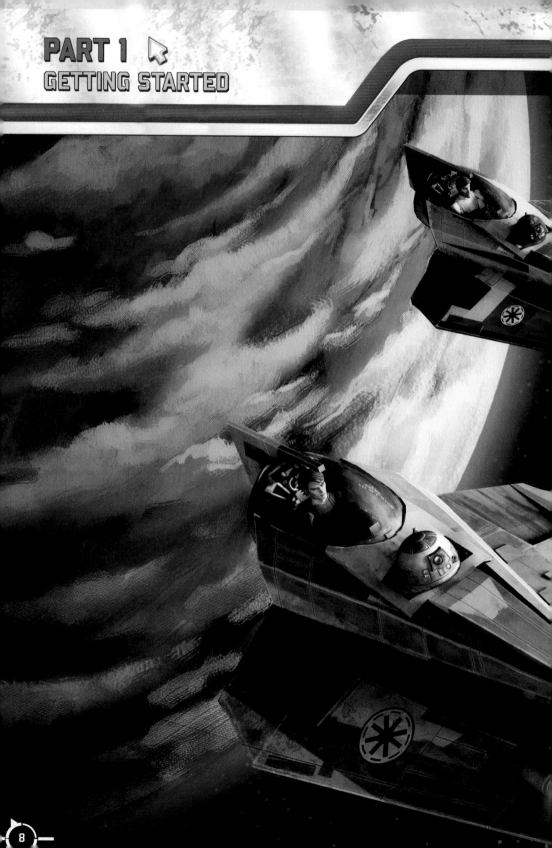

As the Clone Wars rage on across the galaxy, a group of the Republic's greatest heroes gather to greet a new and promising member of the Jedi Order . . .

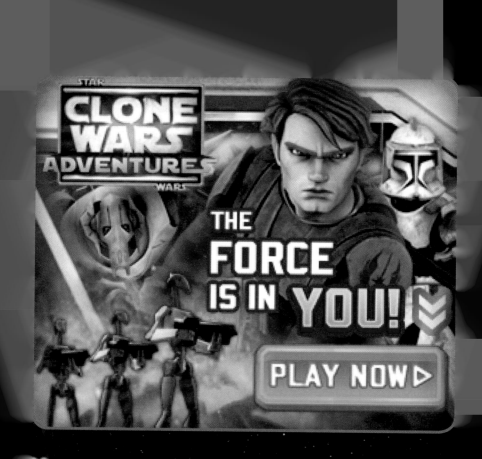

Star Wars®: Clone Wars Adventures™ is an online world where you can battle Separatist enemies and meet the heroes of *Star Wars®: The Clone Wars™*, the hit animated series. In *Clone Wars Adventures* you become a Jedi Knight or Clone Trooper and interact with other players just like you! Play mini-games to earn trophies and credits, customize your character with armor and gear, hang out in your own private house, or chat and make new friends! The Republic needs you, so report to Coruscant for immediate duty!

Code of Conduct

Clone Wars Adventures is a fun place to play games and meet friends. The Code of Conduct helps make sure that everyone stays safe and everyone has a good time!

Top Secret! When you're in *Clone Wars Adventures*, you're a Jedi or Clone Trooper in a galaxy far, far away. Never tell anyone your real name, not even your in-game friends. If someone asks for your name, hometown, phone number, or password, contact a Counselor.

Respect Other Players. Jedi and Clone Troopers treat their comrades with respect, and you should, too. Always talk to other players in the same way you want them to talk to you.

Bad Language Will Be Disintegrated! If you're already treating other players with respect, then there's no need for bad language. Most language of this type is automatically filtered. Remember, you can lose your character for violating this policy!

Cheaters Never Prosper. Cheating in games or tricking your friends to get an edge is forbidden. Anybody who cheats can be suspended or expelled from the game.

Don't Abuse the Naming Policy. We're happy to help you pick a name for your character, but names that violate the Code of Conduct will be changed to something more appropriate. Choose carefully!

Choosing a Name

It's easy to get a cool, *Star Wars*®–sounding name by clicking Suggest Name during character creation. If you want a custom name, just type something new.

ENTER A NAME FOR YOUR CHARACTER:

Character First Name
Rhalia

Character Last Name
Rangeseeker

SUGGEST NAME   OK

Your name will then be reviewed before you can use it.

Off-Limits:

- For your safety, never use your real name as your character name.

- You can use a first name from the *Star Wars*® movies (like Anakin) or a last name (like Calrissian), but not both! Misspellings like "Skiwalker" count, too.

- Inappropriate names that use bad language, reference drugs or alcohol, or mention the titles of other video games aren't allowed. Random gibberish won't work, either, and your first or last name can't be a number.

- If your custom name is judged off-limits, you will be given the random name assigned to you during character creation.

Getting Started

To jump right into the world of *Clone Wars Adventures*, go to clonewarsadventures.com.

Your computer will need an Internet connection. On the main screen, click Sign Up.

You can start customizing your character by using the arrows. Choose your gender, species (human, clone, or Twi'lek), and style. Pick a character that matches your personality or be somebody completely different for a change!

Type in your character's name or click Suggest Name if you want some *Star Wars®* ideas.

Select your country and create a username for your account. The username is separate from your character name. You will need to input it every time you go to the website to log in to *Clone Wars Adventures*.

ALMOST THERE... STAY ON TARGET!

CREATE A LOGIN NAME:

CREATE A PASSWORD:

PARENT'S EMAIL:

☑ I have read and I accept the Terms of Service and Privacy Policy.

OK

RUSH HETASHINE

Create a password. Your password is linked to your username, and you will need to input it every time you start up the game at clonewarsadventures.com. For security reasons, your password needs to be at least eight characters long and contain at least one number. Don't forget your password!

CREATE A PASSWORD:

Enter your e-mail address or a parent's e-mail address. *Clone Wars Adventures* will never give your e-mail address out to anyone!

PARENT'S EMAIL:

If you agree to the terms of service and privacy policy, check the box and click OK. Once you've read and agreed to the end user agreement, click Accept.

☑ I have read and I accept the Terms of Service and Privacy Policy.

You're finished! You can now download and play the game.

The game should download automatically. If not, your web browser may ask you whether you want to install the plug-in. Click Accept or Continue and the download should start. If you're having trouble, check the articles at help.clonewarsadventures. com/app/answers/list/c/3839/.

When the game launches, watch the intro video in which Yoda, Anakin Skywalker, Mace Windu, Ahsoka Tano, and other familiar faces welcome you to the Jedi Temple. As a hero of the Republic, you will play a crucial role in the fight against Count Dooku and the Separatist battle Droids. After the Jedi introduce the basic concepts of playing games, earning credits, and relaxing in your private quarters, they have a gift for you—your first Lightsaber!

Welcome to the Jedi Temple!

Jedi Knights and Clone Troopers rush around in this busy hub of activity. As a new player, you'll land in the Shops area. Let's look around!

Click the floor in front of your character to have him or her run in that direction or you can move around by using the arrow keys. Press the space bar to activate your Lightsaber and take a couple of practice swings!

The people you meet in the Jedi Temple are either fellow players like you or computer-controlled, non-player characters. Other players have names above their heads. Click on these players to bring up a menu that will allow you to access their profiles.

Ranulph Archtracer

SHOPS

Ranulph Archtracer

Some of the non-player characters are happy to talk to you. If you place your cursor over these characters, the cursor icon will change to a rectangular speech bubble. Lots of famous Jedi are here in the Temple, so walk around and try to meet them all!

Click any door to automatically move to the next room. For more on what you can find inside the Jedi Temple, see the section beginning on p. 36.

Using Your Interface

On your screen are buttons that control the different features of *Clone Wars Adventures*. Learn these shortcuts and you'll be an expert in no time.

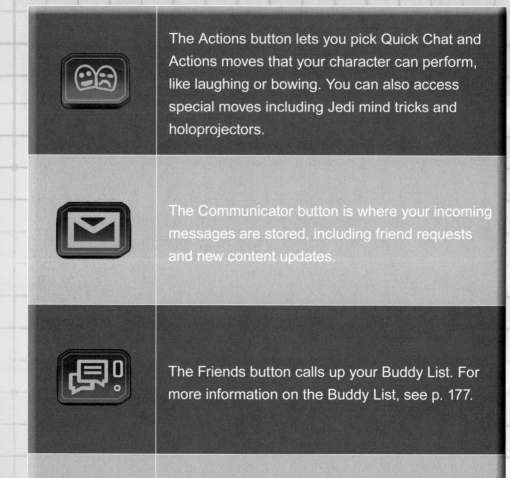

The Actions button lets you pick Quick Chat and Actions moves that your character can perform, like laughing or bowing. You can also access special moves including Jedi mind tricks and holoprojectors.

The Communicator button is where your incoming messages are stored, including friend requests and new content updates.

The Friends button calls up your Buddy List. For more information on the Buddy List, see p. 177.

Type inside the Chat Bar and hit enter to say something to all nearby players.

Click My House to bring up the House Select screen if you want to teleport home.

The Gear button shows your inventory and provides a shortcut to the Store.

The green arrow brings up the complete menu of mini-games in *Clone Wars Adventures*. Have fun!

27,146   200

Your current balances of Republic credits and Station Cash are displayed here. For more information, see p. 138.

You can change the Game Settings here. For more information, see p. 24.

This button gives you a reminder of how to use the interface and lets you contact a Counselor if you need more support.

Use this button to change between full-screen or windowed mode.

Click X to exit the game.

Click your picture to access your profile. For more information on your profile, see p. 26.

The Pets! button lets you summon a Droid companion.

Have some Station Cash and don't know what to spend it on? This button shows the Store items available with Station Cash.

To enter the World and Squad chat screens, click on the green plus sign.

When there is a special event—either a sale or new content—a button will appear to the right of your name and profile picture within the game. Pressing that button will direct the player to the cool, new content or featured items!

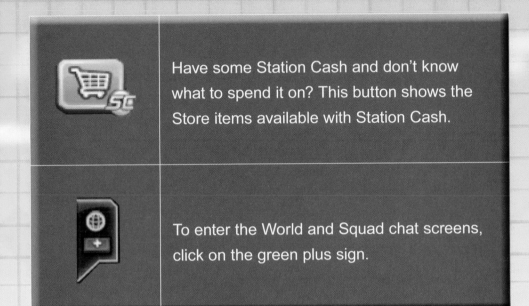

Game Options

You can customize your  *Clone Wars Adventures* experience in lots of ways. Click the wrench icon at the top right to bring up the Game Options menu.

You can play in six different languages: Spanish (Castillian), Spanish (North American), French, German, Portuguese (Brazilian), and English!

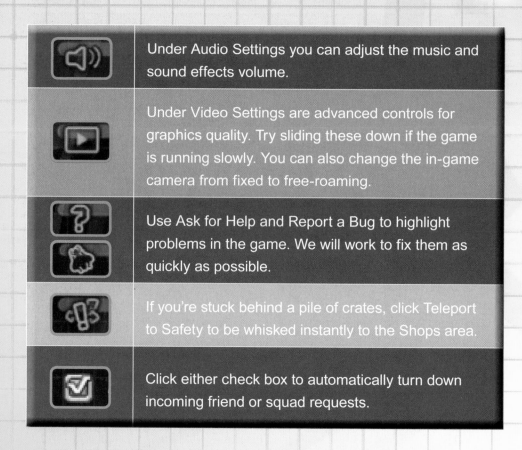

🔊	Under Audio Settings you can adjust the music and sound effects volume.
▶	Under Video Settings are advanced controls for graphics quality. Try sliding these down if the game is running slowly. You can also change the in-game camera from fixed to free-roaming.
❓	Use Ask for Help and Report a Bug to highlight problems in the game. We will work to fix them as quickly as possible.
⚙	If you're stuck behind a pile of crates, click Teleport to Safety to be whisked instantly to the Shops area.
☑	Click either check box to automatically turn down incoming friend or squad requests.

World Chat Here...

GAME OPTIONS
SELECT YOUR OPTIONS

- AUDIO SETTINGS »
- VIDEO SETTINGS »
- ASK FOR HELP »
- TELEPORT TO SAFETY »
- REPORT A BUG »

☐ AUTO DENY FRIEND REQUESTS
☐ AUTO DENY SQUAD REQUESTS

EXIT GAME

DONE ✓

Your Profile

Your profile is a great way to tell other *Clone Wars Adventures* players about yourself and to quickly learn more about other people you meet! Under your profile

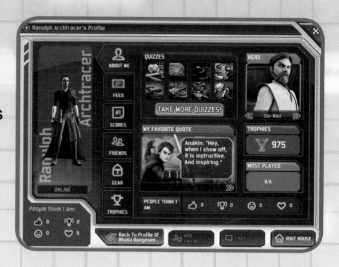

you can show off your coolest gear, display your top scores in mini-games, and take personality quizzes.

To call up your profile, simply click the small picture of your character in the upper left. Another way to view your profile is to click the Friends button at the bottom of the main screen, then click the middle button at the bottom of your Buddy List.

If you're viewing someone else's profile, click the buttons at the bottom to make a friend request, open a chat window, or ask for an invitation to visit their house!

The first page of your profile is called About Me. Just like it says, this is a great spot to tell other players what makes you tick!

Under Quizzes, click the green button to answer the questions and show off your results. What kind of *Star Wars*® animal are you? What color Lightsaber should you carry? You won't know until you take the quizzes!

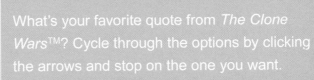

What's your favorite quote from *The Clone Wars*™? Cycle through the options by clicking the arrows and stop on the one you want.

Who's your hero? Whether you prefer the light side or the dark side, your choice of hero says a lot about you. You can pick Commander Cody, General Grievous, or even Jar Jar Binks!

Your Trophy Score is based on how much progress you've made toward earning mini-game trophies. You can learn more about trophies on p. 62.

Have a game you're addicted to? It will show up under Most Played!

Recognizing Fun Players

On your profile is a line reading "People

Think I Am." This is where you'll see the results when other players give you a virtual thumbs-up!

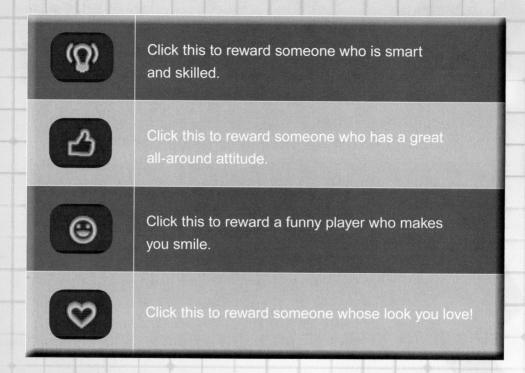

Click this to reward someone who is smart and skilled.	
Click this to reward someone who has a great all-around attitude.	
Click this to reward a funny player who makes you smile.	
Click this to reward someone whose look you love!	

If you don't have any scores yet, be sure to reward other players and ask them to return the favor! You can do this by clicking characters, opening their profiles, and checking the boxes at the lower left.

Other tabs are accessible on your profile—just click the buttons!

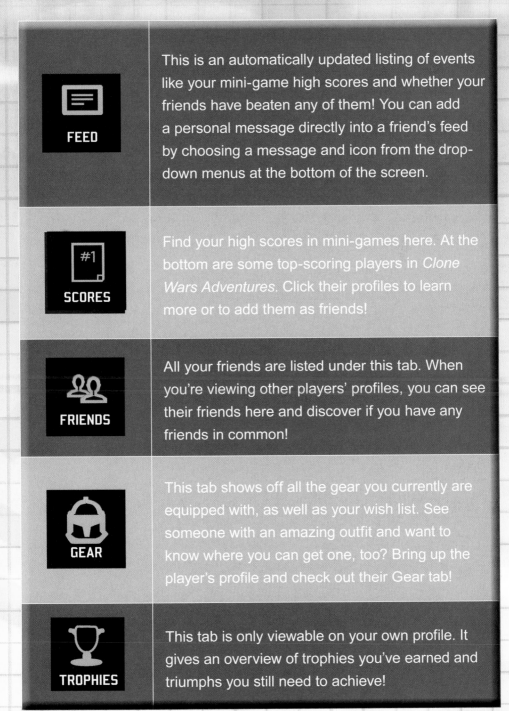

FEED

This is an automatically updated listing of events like your mini-game high scores and whether your friends have beaten any of them! You can add a personal message directly into a friend's feed by choosing a message and icon from the drop-down menus at the bottom of the screen.

SCORES

Find your high scores in mini-games here. At the bottom are some top-scoring players in *Clone Wars Adventures*. Click their profiles to learn more or to add them as friends!

FRIENDS

All your friends are listed under this tab. When you're viewing other players' profiles, you can see their friends here and discover if you have any friends in common!

GEAR

This tab shows off all the gear you currently are equipped with, as well as your wish list. See someone with an amazing outfit and want to know where you can get one, too? Bring up the player's profile and check out their Gear tab!

TROPHIES

This tab is only viewable on your own profile. It gives an overview of trophies you've earned and triumphs you still need to achieve!

Becoming a Jedi Member

When you become a Jedi Member of *Clone Wars Adventures,* you unlock all of the game's premium features. You can play members-only mini-games, get your own deluxe house,

purchase members-only gear, Droids, pets, and vehicles, and even customize your character and Lightsaber!

Ready to join? To purchase a Jedi Membership, click the orange Become a Jedi button at the bottom of the Gear menu or follow the instructions on the *Clone Wars Adventures* website. ⚙ BECOME A JEDI

What does it cost?

1 month	$5.99	or	599 SC
3 months	$14.99	or	1499 SC
6 months	$26.99	or	2699 SC
12 months	$39.99	or	3999 SC
Lifetime	$49.99	or	4999 SC

*Lifetime Memberships indicate the lifetime of the game.

Customizing Your Character and Lightsaber ⚜ Jedi Members only

Jedi Members can change their looks and tune up their Lightsabers under the Gear menu. Just click the Lightsaber or Character Customization buttons.

⚜ Character customization options include new hairstyles, hair colors, eye colors, and skin tones. You can also change your species to human, Twi'lek, Zabrak, Pantoran, and Trandoshan. With a Galactic Passport (see page 34), you can even change your character to Togruta. Different choices have different prices in Republic credits. Click the Apply Now button to save your new look!

⚜ The Lightsaber customization screen lets you work on two Lightsabers at once! First, select the Lightsaber hilt you want to modify. Then choose from different blade colors and shapes, including spiraling beams, sparkling beams, and dark beams! Some Lightsabers have unique crystals. Purchasing new Lightsabers can give you different shapes and special effects.

What's the Galactic Passport?

The Galactic Passport is a package containing amazing *Clone Wars Adventures* rewards, offers, and souvenirs. You can find it at most major stores.

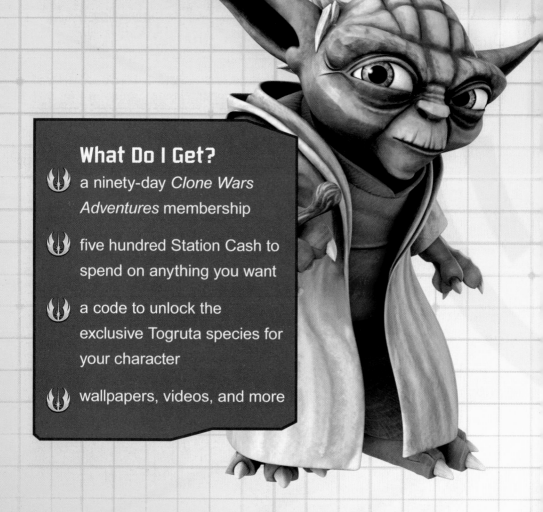

What Do I Get?

- a ninety-day *Clone Wars Adventures* membership

- five hundred Station Cash to spend on anything you want

- a code to unlock the exclusive Togruta species for your character

- wallpapers, videos, and more

You don't *have* to visit the different rooms of the Temple to play games, since the green button on your interface is a handy shortcut for that. But exploring the Temple is a great way to meet other players and soak up the environment of *Clone Wars Adventures*. Read on for the deluxe tour!

TIPS:

FOLLOW THESE SUGGESTIONS

- To get a better view of the Temple, call up Game Options. Under Video Settings, click Use Free Camera.

- Place your cursor over the signs above each doorway and you'll see the games and characters inside that chamber.

- If you run into a glowing globe, click it! It might give you free Republic credits.

- You can teleport to your quarters at any time by clicking the My House button.

Main Hall

Here's where the action is! Since the Main Hall connects to just about every other room in the Temple, expect to see lots of people running back and forth or just hanging out in the roomy center area. During holidays you might see incredible decorations here, like a lighted Life Day tree surrounded by presents!

If you want to meet new friends, the Main Hall is a great place to be. At the lower left-hand corner of your screen, click the green box below the globe icon to bring up the Global Chat window. Talk to other players. If you meet someone you like, call up their profile and send a friend request!

Ranulph Archtracer

Hangar

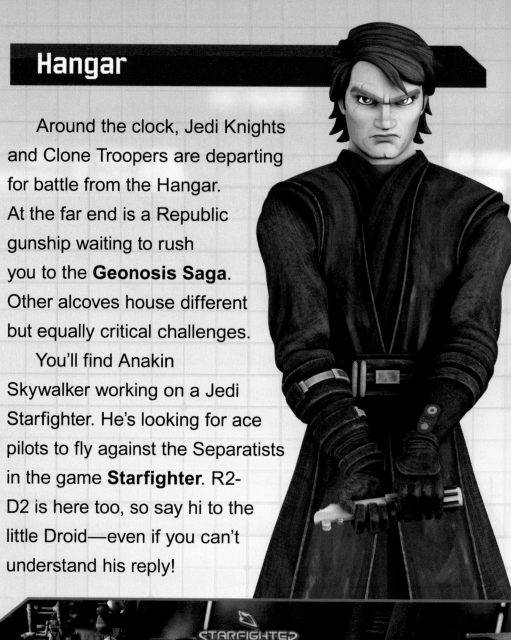

Around the clock, Jedi Knights and Clone Troopers are departing for battle from the Hangar. At the far end is a Republic gunship waiting to rush you to the **Geonosis Saga**. Other alcoves house different but equally critical challenges.

You'll find Anakin Skywalker working on a Jedi Starfighter. He's looking for ace pilots to fly against the Separatists in the game **Starfighter**. R2-D2 is here too, so say hi to the little Droid—even if you can't understand his reply!

STARFIGHTER
Ranulph Archtracer
Anakin Skywalker
R2-D2

Kit Fisto is near the speeders and is ready to challenge you to a round of **Speederbike Racing**. And that's not all— the Separatists are attacking on another front! Jump into a Starfighter and take them out one by one in **Star Typer**.

Training Room

This enormous chamber is where the Republic's finest warriors stay in fighting shape. Adi Gallia is happy to give you a briefing when you walk in the door. Peek over the railing to see Jedi Knights cutting holes in bulkheads and Clone Troopers scrambling over obstacles.

Want to sharpen your own skills? See Obi-Wan Kenobi to be transported to the elevated central platform and battle an opponent in **Lightsaber Duel**.

Throwing your Lightsaber to slice through multiple battle Droids is a critical skill. Luminara Unduli at the room's far end will lead you through **Saber Strike**.

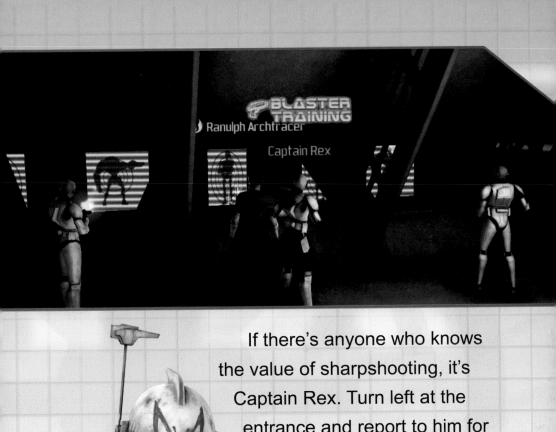

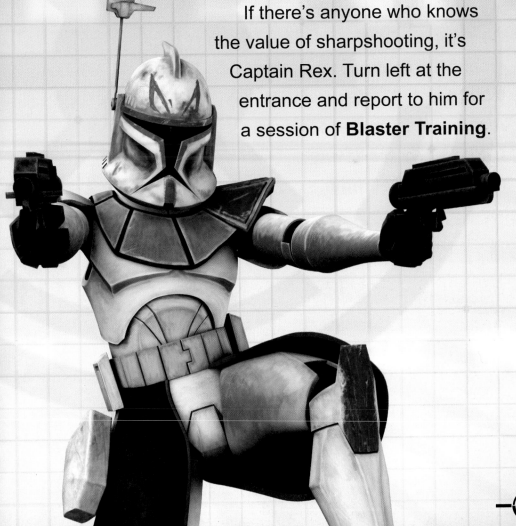

If there's anyone who knows the value of sharpshooting, it's Captain Rex. Turn left at the entrance and report to him for a session of **Blaster Training**.

War Room

The Clone Wars™ is the biggest conflict the galaxy has ever seen! Here in the War Room, top military leaders huddle together to plan their next moves against Count Dooku and General Grievous.

You'll find Admiral Yularen, Commander Cody, and Mace Windu around the holographic strategy table. Talk to Master Windu to receive an assignment to build automated battle towers in **Republic Defender**.

At the far end of the War Room, Plo Koon has an equally urgent mission: An **Attack Cruiser** needs a captain to fight off wave after wave of Separatist warships. Are you prepared to take command?

Lounge

The stress of *The Clone Wars*™ can wear down even the most dedicated solider. Don't let it happen to you! Jedi Knights and Clone Troopers are encouraged to blow off steam in the Lounge when they aren't on missions.

Head to the left when you enter and meet Commander Cards! This clone officer is an expert at **Card Commander** and would love to show you the basics.

At the opposite end of the Lounge are game consoles for **Crisis Ziro**, **Daily Spin**, and

Ranulph Archtracer

Commander Cards

STUNT
GUNGAN

CRISIS
ZIRO

Ranulph Archtracer

Stunt Gungan. Ahsoka Tano and Barriss Offee are having a conversation outside the door to the Officers' Club. They're not allowed inside, but you are—if you're a Jedi Member!

Officers' Club

Only Jedi Members can enter this exclusive, premium club that lies right next to the Lounge. Master Yoda is here, but don't worry—he doesn't want you to get back to work! On the contrary, Yoda wants you to relax and have fun, and the Officers' Club has lots of ways to do just that!

Ranulph Archtracer

Yoda

Ranulph Archtracer

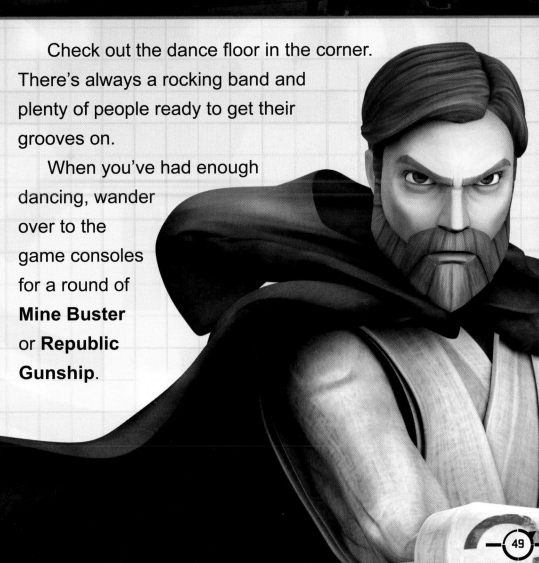

Check out the dance floor in the corner. There's always a rocking band and plenty of people ready to get their grooves on.

When you've had enough dancing, wander over to the game consoles for a round of **Mine Buster** or **Republic Gunship**.

Shops

Here's where you can get a new set of armor, a new Droid, or even your very own Jedi Starfighter. The Shops area is also where players appear in *Clone Wars Adventures* for the first time, so come here if you want to make newcomers feel at home!

Browse the alcoves in this multileveled area to shop for furniture, Jedi gear, Clone Trooper gear, vehicles, speeders, and Droids. Look for doorways that lead to the Workshop, the Archives, and the Lightsaber Construction Chamber.

Ranulph Archtracer GLI-D3
<Vehicles>

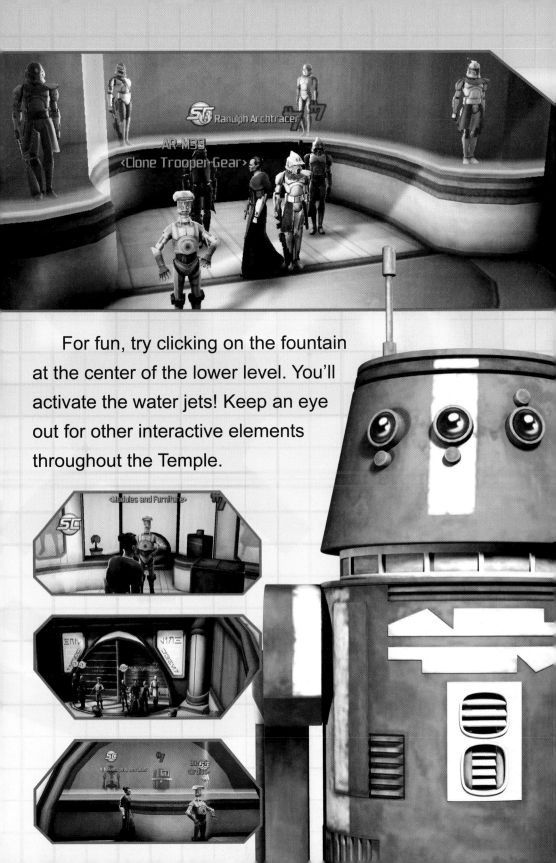

For fun, try clicking on the fountain at the center of the lower level. You'll activate the water jets! Keep an eye out for other interactive elements throughout the Temple.

Archives

The Archives are a welcome change from the busy chaos of the Temple. Here, seekers of wisdom quietly study in the soft glow of thousands of datacards and Holocrons.

You'll find Aayla Secura at the first workstation. She knows that a true Jedi must look beyond surface appearances, and she has long seen the value of the game of **Force Perception**. Give it a try!

Ranulph Archtracer

In the middle of the Archives is the game station for **Daily Trivia**. Here, Jedi Members can demonstrate their knowledge and reaction time.

Chief librarian Jocasta Nu is at the chamber's far end. She will unlock the Holocron vault for Jedi Members who wish to try their luck at the **Daily Holocron**.

Workshop

This cluttered and grease-stained room isn't the prettiest one in the Temple, but for Droid tinkerers it's practically heaven!

Eeth Koth has a report that R2-D2 needs help making it safely through the Coruscant skies to meet Anakin Skywalker. You look like you're good with Droids—can you handle **Rocket Rescue**?

Commander Bly is convinced that fixing Droids' memory banks can help uncover secrets for the war effort. If you have the skills, volunteer for **Droid Programming**!

Droids are great at breaking into security systems, so Commander Gree has agreed to lead a special project. Talk to Gree and report for duty at **Infiltration**!

DROID PROGRAMMING

Commander Bly   Ranulph Archtracer

INFILTRAT

Commander Ga

Lightsaber Construction Chamber

Only Jedi Members can enter this sacred chamber reachable through the Shops area. This is where Jedi students practice aligning Lightsaber crystals into a perfect matrix so they can build weapons to fight the Sith!

Speak to Ki-Adi-Mundi in the center of the chamber and he will explain the importance of **Crystal Attunement**. When you're ready to demonstrate your skills, accept his challenge and improve the Jedi arsenal!

CRYSTAL ATTUNEMENT

Ki-Adi-Mundi

Ranulph Archtracer

>> Not only is it fun to play mini-games, but you earn in-game credits, too! Every game rewards you with Republic credits. The amount of the payout depends on your score and the difficulty setting. Some games, like **Daily Spin**, are completely random! You can check your Republic credits balance in the upper right corner of the screen.

Station Cash: Next to your red Republic credits balance is your Station Cash balance in yellow. You can't earn Station Cash by playing mini-games. To see the ways you can purchase Station Cash, see p. 145.

Trophies

 Mini-games are a fun way to pass time and earn Republic credits, but they can also get you collectible trophies! These are awarded when you beat a certain number of enemies, pass a difficult level, or achieve something else worth celebrating. Most mini-games have their own set of trophies.

 View your Trophy Score under the About Me section of your profile. The harder the trophy is to get, the more points it's worth.

TROPHIES
975

Under the Trophy section of your profile you can see your completed and in-progress trophies. Check out your friends' trophies on their own profiles!

 To see all the available trophies and how to earn them, visit the Trophy Room. Place your cursor over the trophy or its blank outline to get more information about it.

CARD COMMANDER

>> Republic heroes and Separatist villains battle it out in Card Commander. It's up to you to prove you have the card smarts and the deck-building skills to outplay your opponent. Think you're good? Prove it in the tournament!

On the game screen you have several choices:

 Quick Play: Battle another *Clone Wars Adventures* player in a single game.

 Campaign: Play a series of matches against computer-controlled characters from *Star Wars®: The Clone Wars™*.

 Tournament: Compete against some of the very best Card Commander players and win prizes!

 Buy Cards: Make your deck more powerful with a booster pack or Holocron!

 Collection: Review all your cards before you play.

How to Play

Remember: Red cards always beat green cards. Green cards beat blue cards. And blue cards beat red cards. If two cards are the same color, the one with the higher power number inside

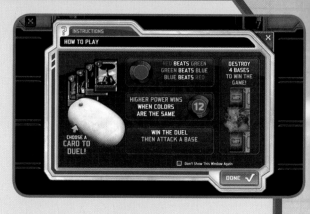

the colored circle will win. If both cards have the same color *and* number, the round is a tie and new cards are chosen.

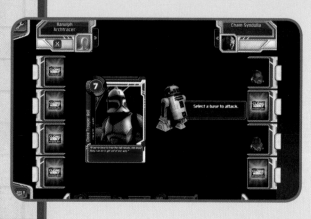

If you win a round, you can target one of the four cards on your opponent's side of the screen for battle. These four cards are bases. If you win, you destroy one of your opponent's bases. Destroy all four to become a Card Commander champion!

The cards at the bottom of the screen make up your hand.

Try to remember the cards that your opponent has, especially the cards protecting his bases. Playing the right color or number at the right moment is the key to victory.

Asajj Ventress
Character · Warrior

When I destroy a base, scan opponent's bases.

Commander Gree
Character · Leader

When I win as a garrison, I stay face up. While I'm face up, all your other blue cards get power +12.

Character · Leader

"Our blockade is impenetrable. When the Republic attacks, they will get quite a surprise."

Holocrons

The cards in your hand are random, but if you have a Holocron, you can make sure a card of your choice stays in your hand for five games or more! You can win Holocrons in card tournaments, get them in booster packs, or buy them in the Store. Use a red pyramid or cube to make a red card stay in your hand, a green pyramid or cube to make a green card stay in your hand, and a blue pyramid or cube to make a blue card stay in your hand.

Ahsoka Tano
Character · Warrior

...adawan learner. I'm

FOLLOW THESE SUGGESTIONS

If you have trouble remembering which colors beat which, the colored circle surrounding the card's power number is a handy reminder.

Memorize the cards of your enemy's bases when they are revealed. You can also get a special card that will shuffle your own bases!

Use Holocrons to keep your best attacking cards in your hand. You can use four cube Holocrons at a time.

Try to take out your opponent's attacking cards. If your last base card is blue, plan ahead to beat all of your opponent's greens!

Pay attention to cards with special abilities. The best cards are found in booster packs.

Want an edge?
Check out the special
Card Commander items
you can get at the Store
with Station Cash:

 Booster packs will give
you stronger cards and
special rewards.

 Silver and gold Holocrons (in both pyramid
and cube shapes) can keep a card in your
hand for up to thirty-five games!

Tournaments

Card Commander tournaments are timed. The
tournament window tells you how much time is left
in the current tournament or when the next one will
begin. You can also check the event calendar to
plan for upcoming tournaments.

The more wins you score in
a tournament, the higher your
position will be and the more prizes you can earn.
Check the leaderboard to see the rankings!

REPUBLIC DEFENDER

>> Battle Droids are on the march! In **Republic Defender**, you are the battlefield commander, placing turrets to wipe out the Droids before they overtake the planet. It's a tricky mix of smart strategy and nonstop action!

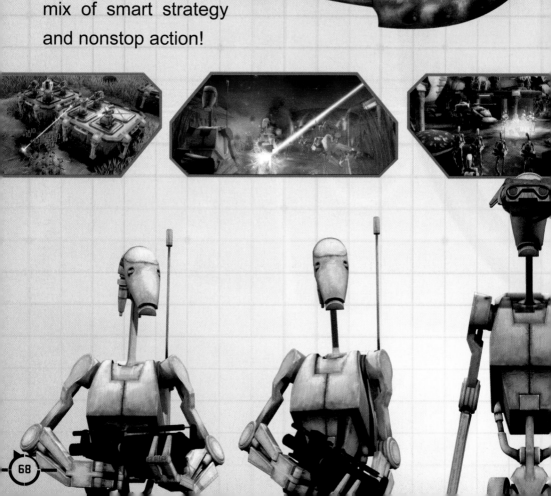

How to Play

The Separatist drop ships are unloading row after row of battle Droids, AAT tanks, and STAP fliers. You have to stop them before they reach the end by building defensive turrets.

Click the tops of the towers that line the Droids' path to select which type of turret you want to build on each tower. Place your cursor over the turret symbol to see its stats and attack range.

Each turret costs energy! You get energy by destroying enemies, and your energy count is displayed at the top right. Turrets can be upgraded to more powerful models, or even sold if you need energy fast! Click the turret and select Upgrade or Sell. Remember, the turret won't work while it's being upgraded!

Enemies attack in waves. You can see what's coming next by viewing the readout at the upper left. Press fast forward if you can't wait to fight the next wave!

Defeated enemies sometimes drop powerups. Click them to pick them up, then click the icon in the powerup bar at the bottom to use them. If an enemy makes it through your defenses, you lose one life.

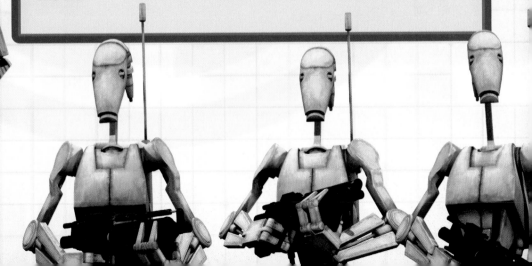

Powerups

Thermal detonator. Makes a big boom!

EMP grenade: This freezes the Droids for a short time.

Seismic charge: Place it on the ground and wait for enemies to travel over it.

Scatter mines: Less powerful than thermal detonators, but with a larger blast area.

Extra life.

Extra energy.

Tank mines: Place these on the path to do extra damage to tanks and less damage to other ground units.

Speeder squad: Calls in a squad of speeders that will hit ground units with blasters and EMP grenades.

Orbital strike: As many turbolaser blasts as you want until the time limit is up.

Y-wing strafing run: Can damage several ground and air units at once.

Jedi heroes: Spawns several Jedi that deal heavy amounts of damage to all ground units.

Turrets

	Blaster Turret: A cheap turret that can hit both ground and air units. Costs 100 energy.
	Repeating Blaster: Fires faster than the regular blaster turret. Costs 150 energy.
	Energy Converter: Doesn't attack, but drains additional energy from Droids that are destroyed in its range. Costs 125 energy.
	Energy Generator: Doesn't attack, but gives you free energy every few seconds. Costs 100 energy.
	Particle Beam: Fires a single beam that causes damage over time. Can hit only ground targets. Costs 175 energy.
	Missile Turret: Fires clusters of missiles at multiple air units. Costs 150 energy.
	Mortar Cannon: Fires long-range exploding mortars at multiple ground units. Costs 200 energy
	Anti-Air Turret: Powerful turret with a long range that can hit only air units. Costs 200 energy.
	Thermal Grenade: Fires an explosive thermal grenade that can hit multiple ground units. Costs 175 energy.
	Power Surger: Doesn't attack, but increases the firepower of the turrets within its range. Costs 175 energy.
	Turbo Laser: A high-powered turret that is great against heavily armored enemies. Costs 250 energy.
	Ion Cannon: Deals heavy damage to shielded enemies. Costs 225 energy.

Turrets (cont)

	Ion Repeater: Similar to the Ion Cannon, but with a longer range and a higher rate of fire. Costs 250 energy.
	Gravity Generator: Decrease the speed of all nearby ground droids. Costs 300 energy.
	ARC Troopers Turret: Ideal for taking down those really tough droids. Costs 300 energy.
	Deactivator: A charged up deactivator can deal a great amount of damage to stronger droids. Costs 375 energy.

⚙ TIPS

FOLLOW THESE SUGGESTIONS

- Press the space bar to see the health of enemy units and the flight paths for STAPs.

- Click any enemy (or turret) for details on that unit.

- Some levels have extra-tough final boss enemies. Be prepared!

- Use the arrows and the plus/minus buttons at the bottom right of your screen to change your view. You can also zoom in and out with your mouse wheel.

SPEEDERBIKE RACING

>> In Speederbike Racing, you take the controls of one of the fastest machines in the galaxy! Race against your friends or computer-controlled players. See if you can beat your top score!

How to Play

The arrow keys or WASD keys let you steer left and right or go faster or slower. Look for boost powerups as you rocket through the course. If you drive through these, you'll get a speed boost and earn one point for your Boost Bar under the speedometer. When you get four boost points, hang on tight—your speederbike gets a superboost! But beware of the purple slowdown pads! The first player to finish the set number of laps is the winner.

You can invite up to three friends to race with you! Just choose Invite Friends after you choose a stage, and then click your online friends to instantly invite them to a race. For more information about inviting your friends to play games, see p. 182.

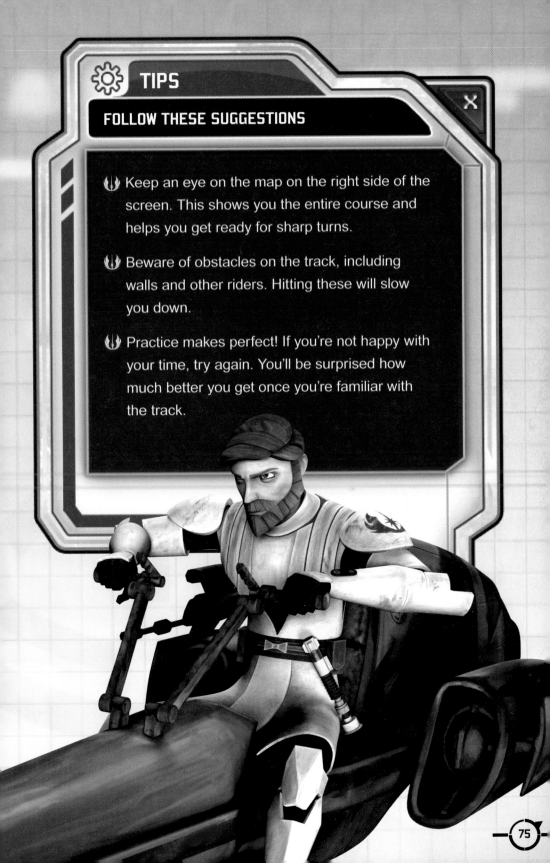

TIPS

FOLLOW THESE SUGGESTIONS

- Keep an eye on the map on the right side of the screen. This shows you the entire course and helps you get ready for sharp turns.

- Beware of obstacles on the track, including walls and other riders. Hitting these will slow you down.

- Practice makes perfect! If you're not happy with your time, try again. You'll be surprised how much better you get once you're familiar with the track.

STARFIGHTER

>> Anakin Skywalker just recruited you as a pilot! Jump into the cockpit of a Jedi Starfighter and take out the Separatists in the skies of strange planets and the darkness of outer space.

How to Play

Enemies will come at you in waves. Fire your lasers with your left mouse button and your missiles with your right button. Enemies are marked with red circles. Hit the X or Z keys to do a barrel roll and avoid enemy fire. Flying through powerups will make your ship stronger and help you complete the mission!

Powerups

	Boosted shield strength
	Score multiplier
	Multi-shot missiles

TIPS

FOLLOW THESE SUGGESTIONS

- Keep an eye on your shield strength at the lower right. If it's red, you can lose a life if you hit anything. Look for powerups or make yourself harder to hit with a barrel roll!

- You can score more points by hitting enemies one after the other. Your combo hits are displayed at the top right.

- Missiles hit their targets automatically and also hit nearby enemies. For best results, fire them at big groups!

- You have to wait for missiles to recharge before firing more. When the missile icon at the lower right is red, fire away!

- Friendly ships are marked with green circles. Don't worry, you can't hurt them. Keep shooting and defeat the Separatists!

SABER STRIKE

>> In Saber Strike, you can throw your Lightsaber to take out dozens of battle Droids at once. Become a one-person wrecking crew!

How to Play

Hold down the left mouse button to powerup your throw and move the mouse to aim. Release the button to send your saber flying!

You can also move your player left and right with the arrow keys. Destroy the listed number of Droids without running out of throws and you win.

TIPS

FOLLOW THESE SUGGESTIONS

- Some levels have powerups such as extra Lightsabers. Hit these as you throw to collect them.

- There's no time limit, so study tricky levels and plan your throws carefully. Experiment with bouncing your Lightsaber off walls and obstacles.

- Catch your Lightsaber after you throw it for bonus points!

LIGHTSABER DUEL

>> The Lightsaber is the weapon of a Jedi Knight. Prove yourself worthy of carrying this elegant energy sword by beating the greatest Jedi in the Order. You can even challenge your friends!

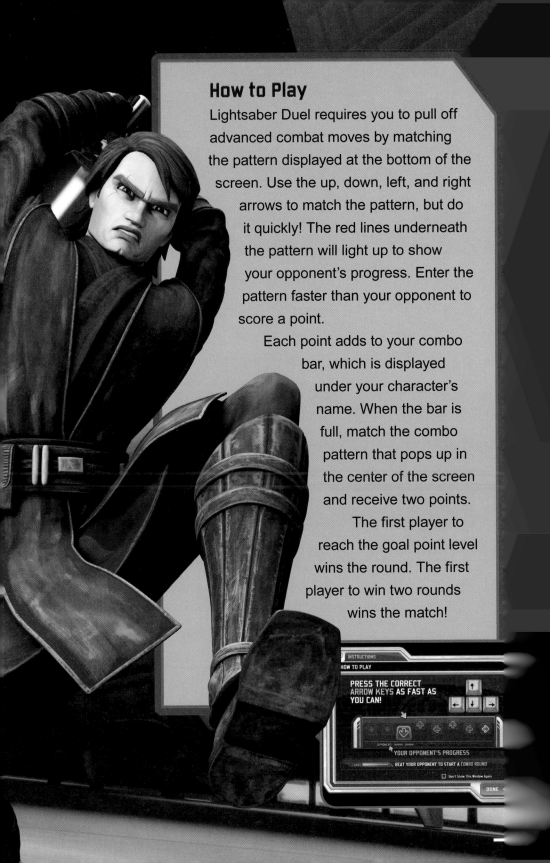

How to Play

Lightsaber Duel requires you to pull off advanced combat moves by matching the pattern displayed at the bottom of the screen. Use the up, down, left, and right arrows to match the pattern, but do it quickly! The red lines underneath the pattern will light up to show your opponent's progress. Enter the pattern faster than your opponent to score a point.

Each point adds to your combo bar, which is displayed under your character's name. When the bar is full, match the combo pattern that pops up in the center of the screen and receive two points.

The first player to reach the goal point level wins the round. The first player to win two rounds wins the match!

INSTRUCTIONS
HOW TO PLAY

PRESS THE CORRECT
ARROW KEYS AS FAST AS
YOU CAN!

OPPONENT:

YOUR OPPONENT'S PROGRESS

COMBO   BEAT YOUR OPPONENT TO START A COMBO ROUND

☐ Don't Show This Window Again

DONE

TIPS

FOLLOW THESE SUGGESTIONS

🌀 Invite a friend to battle by selecting multiplayer from the Stage Select screen. For help on inviting friends to play games, see p. 182.

🌀 Move fast, but be careful. If you make a mistake, you have to start the pattern over again from the beginning.

🌀 Lightsaber Duel lets you see the fighting styles of your favorite characters from *Star Wars®: The Clone Wars™*. You'll battle Anakin Skywalker, Ahsoka Tano, Plo Koon, and more.

🌀 Different Lightsabers let you use different combat styles. Experiment with a few to find the one that suits you!

DROID PROGRAMMING

Jedi Members only

>> Droids like R2-D2 need tune-ups, and Droid Programming is just what the mechanic ordered! Stack blocks of the same color to remove them from the Droid memory banks.

How to Play

Click the left mouse button to grab blocks of the same color, and move the mouse to put them into a different row. Click the right mouse button to release them.

Match four or more blocks of the same color to clear them! Beware of obstacles and try to find special blocks containing powerups.

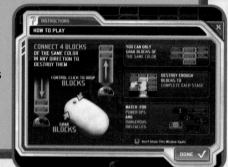

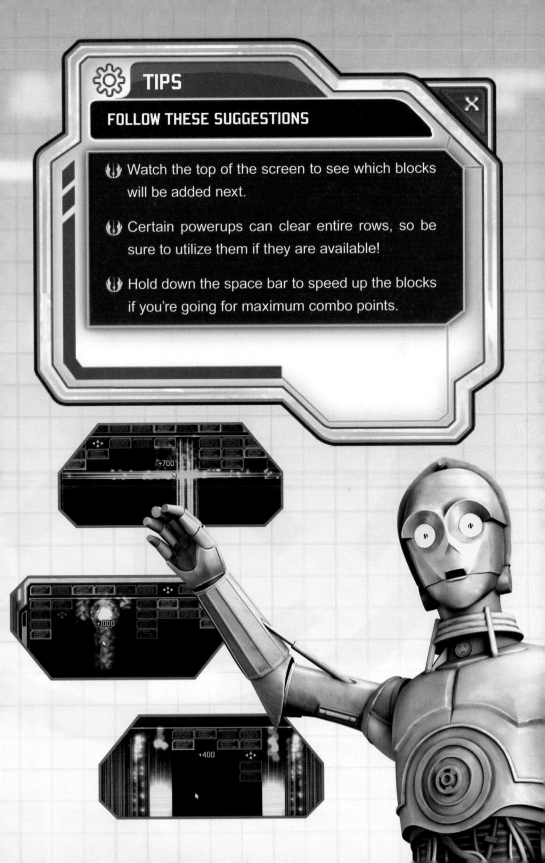

⚙ TIPS

FOLLOW THESE SUGGESTIONS

⚜ Watch the top of the screen to see which blocks will be added next.

⚜ Certain powerups can clear entire rows, so be sure to utilize them if they are available!

⚜ Hold down the space bar to speed up the blocks if you're going for maximum combo points.

+700

+1000

+400

INFILTRATION

>> R2-D2 needs to break into a Separatist security system, and time is running out! Match the colored data orbs into groups by spinning the security ring. Eliminate the orbs and crack the code!

How to Play

New, colored data orbs drop from the top of the screen. Rotate the security ring with the left and right arrow keys to make groupings of same-colored orbs. If three or more data orbs of the same color are touching, they disappear!

The cracked gray orbs can't be matched. You'll have to work around these.

Glowing weak points on the security ring can save you from elimination. If you drop an orb on one of them, *all* orbs of the same color will disappear!

FOLLOW THESE SUGGESTIONS

Orbs have different colors and different patterns. Watch the top of the screen to see which type is coming up next and plan ahead.

Beat the clock! The longer you take, the closer the walls get. Try to eliminate tall structures as quickly as possible.

Higher levels have two security rings. You must first clear the outer ring before you can work on the true target.

Don't speed! It can be hard to control the ring if you're spinning it quickly. Place your data orbs carefully!

You can also clear orbs of a different color if they're touching your matched set of orbs (and not touching anything else).

Stage 21

SCORE

500

FORCE PERCEPTION

Jedi Members only

>> Are you as observant as the greatest Jedi Masters? Prove it with Force Perception!

How to Play

You will see two pictures that look identical, but they're not! Find the five differences between the pictures and click them before time runs out. If you're stuck, click the Force Sense button to get a hint.

? INSTRUCTIONS
HOW TO PLAY ✕

FIND THE
5 DIFFERENCES
BETWEEN THE TWO PICTURES

WATCH THE TIMER!
FIND THEM FAST FOR
MORE POINTS!

1:50

CLICK ON
DIFFERENCES

FORCE SENSE BUTTON
MUST RECHARGE AFTER USE
Force Sense

CLICK
Force Sense
FOR HINTS

EACH PICTURE WILL HAVE
NEW DIFFERENCES
EVERY TIME YOU PLAY

☐ Don't Show This Window Again

TIPS

FOLLOW THESE SUGGESTIONS

⚜ You lose points if you click the wrong spot, so be very sure of your choices!

⚜ You can click either the top or bottom picture to record the differences that you've spotted.

⚜ You need to wait for the Force Sense bar to recharge before you can use it again.

⚜ The differences change around every time. Just because you've seen a picture before, it doesn't mean the answers are the same!

X

Round Completed!

Round Time:	35
Force Sense Uses:	0
Bad Guesses:	0
Round	/688
Total Score	17688

Trophy Earned!
Jedi Seer

QUIT

NEXT

A STAR TYPER

✦ Jedi Members only

In Star Typer, your quickness with a keyboard is the only thing that can stop the Separatist squadrons! The advancing enemies have letters on them, and typing those letters will move your ship into position and fire its lasers. But be careful—type the wrong keys too many times and you're done for!

How to Play

As soon as a Separatist Starfighter appears at the top of the screen, type that letter to destroy it. The longer you take, the closer the enemies get! The right side of the screen records your score, your hit streak, and your score multiplier for long hit streaks.

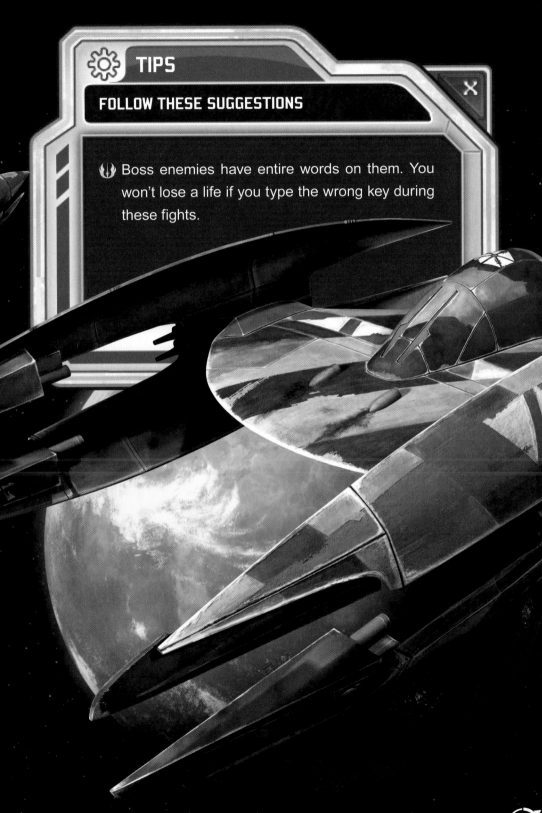

⚙ TIPS

FOLLOW THESE SUGGESTIONS

Boss enemies have entire words on them. You won't lose a life if you type the wrong key during these fights.

X

STUNT GUNGAN

>> Jar Jar Binks is always crashing into things. In Stunt Gungan, use Jar Jar's natural clumsiness to set a new galactic record!

How to Play

Aim the arrow to select the angle of Jar Jar's launch. To make him go really far, wait until the arrow is completely lit up. Jar Jar will keep going if he hits a floating Droid, a box of explosives, a repulsor platform, or other objects. He'll stop if he hits a mud puddle or pile of gunk.

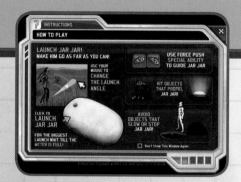

⚙ TIPS

FOLLOW THESE SUGGESTIONS

☖ Use Force-push to keep Jar Jar going! You start with three up and three down Force-pushes. Try using a down push to shove Jar Jar into a box of explosives!

☖ Collect more Force-push powerups in the sky. Try to beat your best distance!

Force Push Down +1

ROCKET RESCUE

R2-D2 is loyal and brave, and in Rocket Rescue he needs your help! Anakin Skywalker is waiting for R2 to meet him at the landing pad. But R2's rocket boosters are low on fuel and the skies of Coruscant aren't exactly friendly!

How to Play

Using your arrow keys, move R2-D2 up, down, left, and right. The direction of your goal is marked by an arrow at the top center of the screen. Flying uses up fuel, and hitting obstacles does, too.

The fuel bar on the right will warn you when you're running low. If R2 runs out, he falls and you lose one life. You can get more fuel, bonus points, or extra lives by collecting glowing powerups throughout the level.

TIPS

FOLLOW THESE SUGGESTIONS

X

- Watch out for enemies! Buildings and speeders will just get in your way, but probe Droids and electrical force fields will zap you!

- Repulsors can be your friend. These glowing platforms act as trampolines, giving you a big boost without using any fuel. Just be sure you hit them at the right angle!

- Take a break! You can rest on some platforms if you want to take time to plan your next move.

- Collect them all! The top right of your screen displays the number of possible powerups in the level. Don't be afraid to explore.

- Want a top score? You get bonus points for the amount of fuel left in your tanks when you finish the level.

Powerups

+10		Ten bonus points
+30		Thirty bonus points
		One extra life
		More rocket fuel

BLASTER TRAINING

Jedi Members only

>> Clone Troopers spend hours every day in the Blaster Training chamber. Are you as good at sharpshooting as Captain Rex?

How to Play

Use your mouse to aim your blaster at the targets in the firing range, and click the left mouse button to shoot. Holographic battle Droids will slide along the tracks between doorways and pop up from behind objects.

Practice hitting the Droids in the head to score critical hits and rack up bonus points. Critical hits will also take out super battle Droids with one shot instead of two!

If a green Jedi or Clone Trooper hologram appears, hold your fire! Hitting these targets will subtract points from your score. Beat the score goal without running out of time to move to the next level!

BLASTER TRAINING

Ranulph Archtracer

Captain Rex

FOLLOW THESE SUGGESTIONS

After passing round three, round six, and round ten, you'll get a bonus round! Keep the Droid parts in the air by blasting them.

Your accuracy score is the percentage of hits compared to misses. See how close you can get to 100 percent!

Targets at the far end of the firing range are smaller and harder to hit. If you're having trouble, concentrate on the easier, closer targets first.

Critical hits are important! Their score multiplier effect will help you finish the level.

If you pass the score goal for each level and there's still time remaining, relax! You've already won, so have fun until the clock runs out.

DAILY SPIN

Daily Spin is a fun, surprising way for all players to earn some quick Republic credits. Take a spin, take a chance—and win big!

How to Play

Click the green button at the bottom left to start the wheel turning. As each ring locks into position, it selects a new number. If you're really lucky and all four rings have high numbers, you can get a huge payout!

TIPS

FOLLOW THESE SUGGESTIONS

The wheel is completely random, so don't worry about special techniques.

Like the name says, you can play Daily Spin only once per day. If you're disappointed in your winnings, don't feel bad. Just try again tomorrow!

ATTACK CRUISER

>> You can prove your valor in combat with Attack Cruiser. As the captain of a Republic warship, you issue the commands to steer the mighty vessel and fire its weapons. The Separatists are attacking! All hands on deck!

How to Play

You can take your Attack Cruiser inside the battlefield ring with the arrow or WASD keys. Use your mouse to aim your laser cannons and the left mouse button to fire them.

Some enemies will drop powerups. Steer your ship over these to pick them up. If you get a Special Attack, use your right mouse button to unleash it. Survive all the enemy waves and you'll be a hero of the Republic!

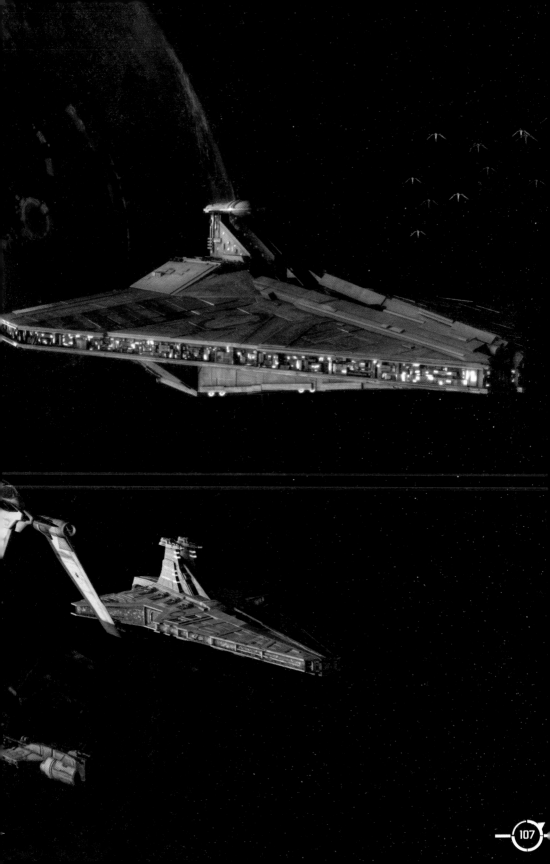

TIPS

FOLLOW THESE SUGGESTIONS

X

- Keep moving! A stationary ship is a sitting duck. Remember, you can fire in any direction while you're moving, even behind you.

- Red arrows around your ship show the directions that enemy attacks are coming from.

- Don't leave the battlefield! The glowing ring represents the battle arena. You will be warned if you travel too far in one direction.

- Your shield meter is in the bottom right corner. If it turns yellow, you're at half strength, and if it's red, your ship is in serious trouble.

- Separatist Starfighters are fast. Aim in front of their paths so they'll fly right into your laser fire.

- Powerups are key to your combat survival. Always pick them up!

Powerups

	Shield boost
	Weapons upgrade
	V-Torrent attack run
	Extra life
	Scatter mine
	EMP (Electromagnetic Pulse) attack
	Invulnerability

CRYSTAL ATTUNEMENT

Jedi Members only

>> In Crystal Attunement, Jedi Members can achieve true mastery by aligning the crystals used to build Lightsabers. Link the colors before you use up all your turns!

How to Play

When you start, one crystal in the grid will be white. Look at the colors of the crystals touching that one, and select one of those colors using the buttons at the lower right. Those colored crystals will turn white, too. Repeat until all the crystals are attuned.

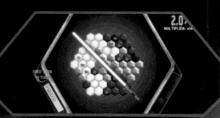

⚙ TIPS

FOLLOW THESE SUGGESTIONS

- Plan ahead! Study the crystal grid and think about your next two or three moves at once.

- Look for crystals that give you powerups.

- On the higher difficulties, you lose a turn if you run out of time!

REPUBLIC GUNSHIP

 Jedi Members only

>> In this action game for Jedi Members, you control a Republic gunship during the Battle of Geonosis. Separatist enemies will come at you from above, below, and even from behind. Use all your weapons to blast the Separatists from the battlefield!

How to Play

Use the WASD keys to move your gunship left, right, up, and down. Use the left mouse button (or the spacebar) to fire your weapons. Collecting powerups will improve your weapons systems and allow you to destroy multiple enemies at once.

Watch out for laser fire and obstacles, and keep your eye on the health bar at the top right of your screen. Stay alive until the last enemy is defeated!

Powerups

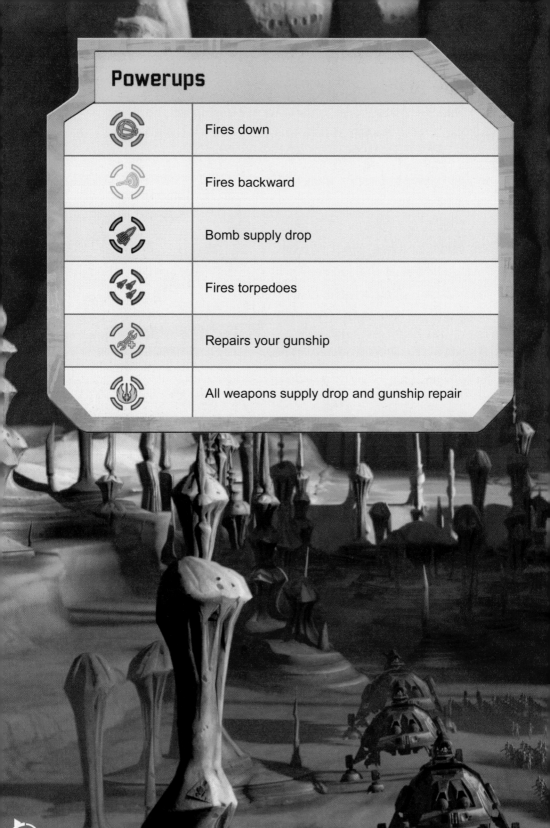	Fires down
	Fires backward
	Bomb supply drop
	Fires torpedoes
	Repairs your gunship
	All weapons supply drop and gunship repair

TIPS

FOLLOW THESE SUGGESTIONS

- Powerups are the key to victory. The bottom of the screen shows how many of each attack you have remaining. Collect more powerups to recharge.

- Several times during the game, friendly gunships will appear to give you full recharges.

- Study the Separatist enemies to see what kinds of powerups they drop. If you're running low on health, battle Droids on the ground usually drop orange repair powerups.

- You can run into enemies to destroy them, but you'll take damage, too!

DAILY HOLOCRON

Jedi Members only

>> The Daily Holocron is your chance to unlock the great treasures of the Jedi. Holocrons normally store wisdom and secrets, and the ones in this game can also give you lots of Republic credits!

How to Play

Each day, a different column of Holocrons will light up. Click one of the four Holocrons in that column, then click again to stop it from spinning. You can win hundreds of credits!

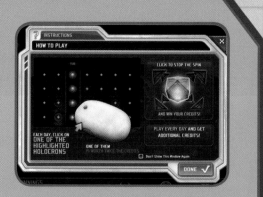

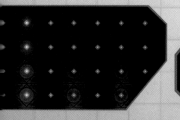

Click On The Holocron!

"Evil is not born, it is taught."

TIPS

FOLLOW THESE SUGGESTIONS

- You can only play once per day, but for each day of the week you play, you'll get bonus credits.

- One Holocron per day will pay out double the credits!

- After you collect your winnings, you'll see a famous Jedi quote. Study these to become as wise as Master Yoda!

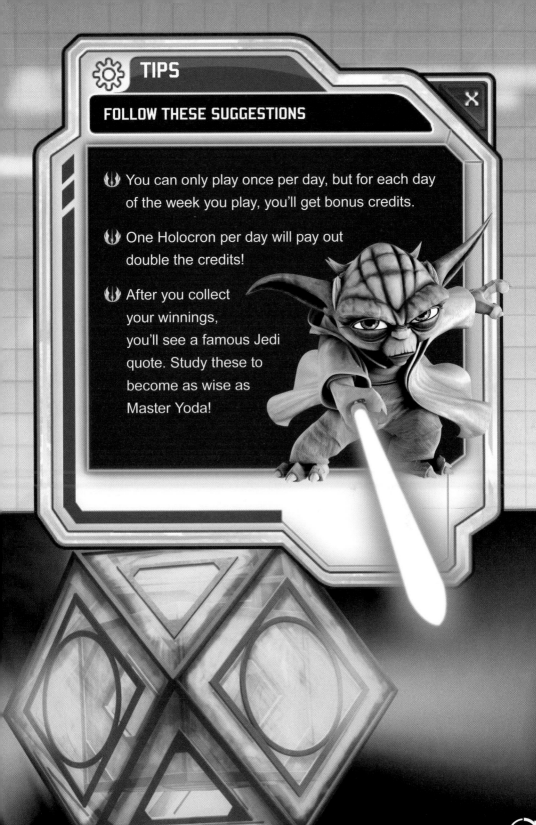

DAILY TRIVIA

Jedi Members only

>> In Daily Trivia, Jedi Members can show off their knowledge of *Star Wars®: The Clone Wars*™ to win Republic credits!

How to Play

Five questions are offered every day, with four possible answers for each. Correct answers on the first try are worth credits! Each wrong answer will take away credits. Answer well and answer fast—you'll earn extra credits if you beat the Speed Bonus timer!

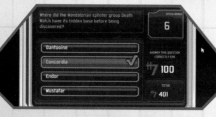

⚙ TIPS

FOLLOW THESE SUGGESTIONS

⚜ Take your time! You can win more credits if you beat the Speed Bonus timer, but that won't matter if you get the answers wrong!

⚜ All the questions are from *The Clone Wars*™, so it helps to go back and watch older episodes, too!

X

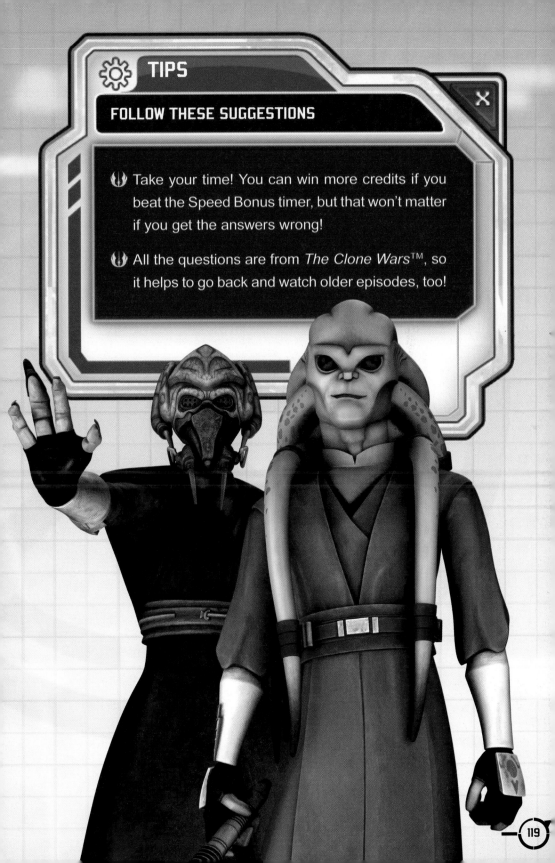

MINE BUSTER

🌀 Jedi Members only

▶▶ In Mine Buster, Jedi Members have a vital mission—clear the Republic supply lines of drifting Separatist mines! By dropping seismic charges, you can trigger a chain reaction of explosions and make space safe for ships once again.

How to Play

Click a point on the screen to drop a seismic charge in that spot. Every mine caught in an explosion will make its own explosion, hopefully clearing even more mines! Clear the listed number of mines to advance to the next level.

FOLLOW THESE SUGGESTIONS

- Red mines make the biggest explosions, and green mines make the smallest.

- Asteroids and enemy Starfighters don't make explosions, but you still earn points for destroying them.

- Look for extra seismic-charge powerups on some levels.

- There's no time limit, so study the screen carefully!

CRISIS ZIRO

Jedi Members only

Ziro the Hutt is free from prison, and Cad Bane is speeding him to safety. Control Quinlan Vos and stop the fleeing outlaws. It's Crisis Ziro!

How to Play

You must jump from speeder to speeder in the busy Coruscant skylanes to reach Ziro and Cad Bane. Aim the arrow around Quinlan with your mouse and left-click to jump in that direction.

You get points for jumping on speeders and extra points for jumping over them! Keep moving to the right or the slow-moving traffic will carry you off the left-hand side of the screen and make you fall. When you reach Ziro and Cad Bane, you've won the level!

You also have a time limit, which you can check with the timer bar in the upper right corner of the screen. You can get more time by jumping on gold speeders.

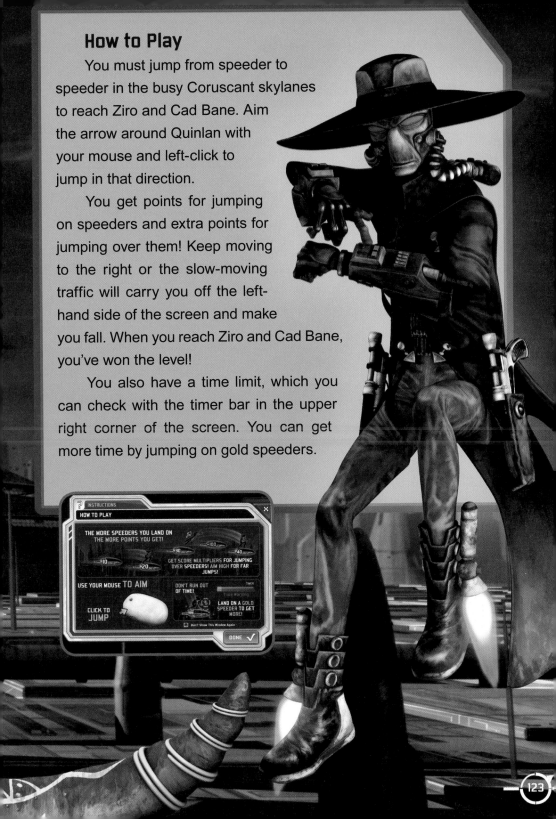

INSTRUCTIONS

HOW TO PLAY

THE MORE SPEEDERS YOU LAND ON THE MORE POINTS YOU GET!

+30   +100   +40

+10   +20   GET SCORE MULTIPLIERS FOR JUMPING OVER SPEEDERS! AIM HIGH FOR FAR JUMPS!

USE YOUR MOUSE TO AIM   DON'T RUN OUT OF TIME!   TIMER

CLICK TO JUMP   LAND ON A GOLD SPEEDER TO GET MORE!

Don't Show This Window Again

DONE ✓

Helps and Hazards

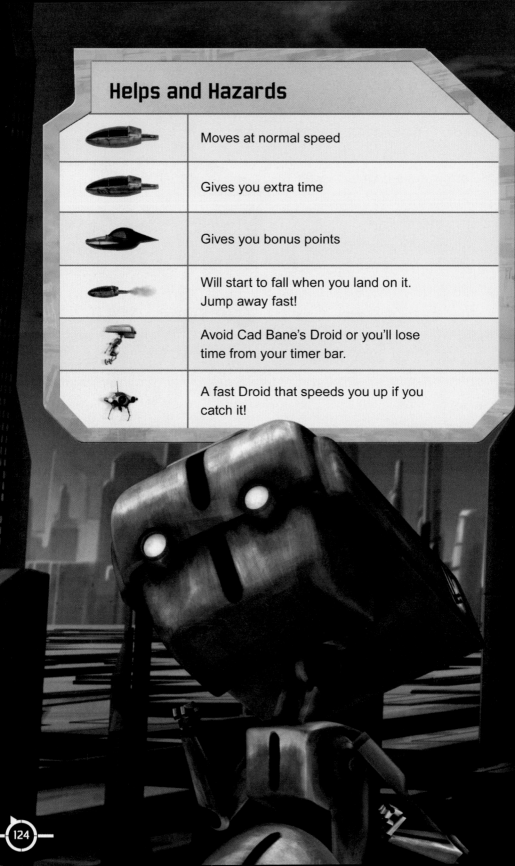	Moves at normal speed
	Gives you extra time
	Gives you bonus points
	Will start to fall when you land on it. Jump away fast!
	Avoid Cad Bane's Droid or you'll lose time from your timer bar.
	A fast Droid that speeds you up if you catch it!

TIPS

FOLLOW THESE SUGGESTIONS

Build up a score bonus by jumping on lots of speeders in a row. You get the biggest scores by jumping over speeders.

Each difficulty setting has ten levels. Beat all ten and then try a harder setting!

>> *The Clone Wars*™ began on Geonosis, and now it's time to return! The rocky homeworld of the insectoid Geonosians churns out thousands of battle Droids every day. The Republic has planned a second attack to shut down the Droid foundries once and for all, and Captain Breaker needs a hotshot pilot behind the controls!

See Breaker to report for duty, and you will be taken to the bridge of the Attack Cruiser leading the assault. You will receive your orders directly from Obi-Wan Kenobi and Admiral Yularen.

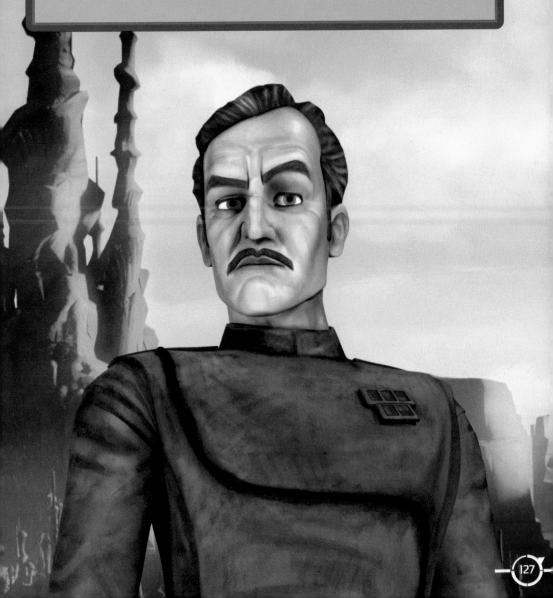

How to Play

If you've already logged time in the cockpit playing Starfighter, you'll be familiar with the basic control systems of the first level. You fly your attack craft using the mouse to avoid incoming fire and to aim. Separatist enemies will be marked with red icons. Fire your laser cannons with your left mouse button and use your right button to release missiles. Listen to your mission commander and keep the skies clear for the Republic gunships!

TIPS

FOLLOW THESE SUGGESTIONS

- Collect powerups to repair your shields and upgrade your blasters.

- Stay out of the line of fire by hitting the Z and X keys to do a barrel roll.

- There's no limit on lasers, so fire away!

If you finished the first stage, congratulations! But the Geonosis Saga is just beginning. As you progress through the missions, you'll have the chance to play special levels of games you might already know, including Republic Defender, Republic Gunship, and Saber Strike.

These levels are played using the same controls as in their original games, so check the sections on Republic Defender, Republic Gunship, and Saber Strike if you need a reminder.

But be on the lookout for new developments! The Separatists are desperate to defend Geonosis and have deployed weapons that the Republic's generals have never seen before. On the Republic Defender levels, for example, you'll have to fight shielded Separatist air units. Luckily, your Clone Troopers are ready to build an all-new ion repeater tower that will swat those pesky Starfighters from the sky!

Make it all the way through the Geonosis Saga and you'll earn a special reward. You'll also receive the title "Hero of Geonosis"!

DARK SIDE DUEL

Jedi Members only

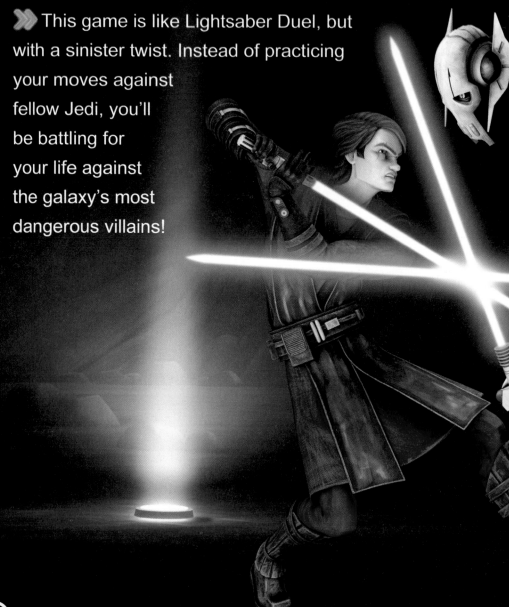

>> This game is like Lightsaber Duel, but with a sinister twist. Instead of practicing your moves against fellow Jedi, you'll be battling for your life against the galaxy's most dangerous villains!

How to Play

From the main screen you'll have the option to play campaign mode or multiplayer. If you select multiplayer, you'll be matched with a random opponent after you choose your difficulty setting.

Campaign mode starts out with Obi-Wan Kenobi leading you through three tutorial sessions. These are designed to get you comfortable with using Force powers. Though the Force powers are new, the basic controls are the same as in Lightsaber Duel. If you need a reminder, check the Lightsaber Duel section.

Force Powers

Force Slow: Adds one more move to a Lightsaber sequence. This makes the sequence take longer to complete and can lead to the other player finishing first.

Force Persuasion: Requires the Lightsaber sequence to be input in reverse order, moving from right to left. This is tricky at first, but with practice you'll get the hang of it!

Force Confusion: The toughest of the Force powers, this requires each Lightsaber move to be input in reverse fashion. If you see an up arrow, hit your down arrow; if you see a right arrow, hit your left arrow. As you can imagine, this can get confusing in the middle of a duel!

TIPS

FOLLOW THESE SUGGESTIONS

In campaign mode, you'll fight General Grievous, Asajj Ventress, Count Dooku, and finally, Savage Opress!

Practice the Force powers in the tutorials before you try to use them against a Separatist warrior.

Remember that Force powers will wear off with time. Check the icon under your status bar to see if your opponent is still using the Force against you!

>> What good is earning Republic credits in mini-games if you don't have something fun to spend them on? The Store is where you turn your credits into awesome armor and devoted Droid pets. Check your Republic credits balance at the upper right of your screen, then shop for items that have their price listed in Republic credits.

19,469   150   [?] [🔧] [◫] [X]

GEAR > STORE > OUTFITS > CLONE TROOPER GEAR   [?] X

< BACK   ⚙ Filters

CLONE SNOWTROOPER

COMMANDER TRAUMA

SCORCH

ARC TROOPER FIVES

BUY! 600

BUY! 300

BUY SET 900

I HAVE 1,000   0

REDEEM A CODE   VIEW WISHLIST   BECOME A JEDI MEMBER >>   ADD STATION CASH >>

Some items can be bought using only Station Cash. These are marked with a yellow Station Cash icon.

Some items are available only to Jedi Members. These are marked with the winged Lightsaber Jedi Member icon.

Using the Store Menu

Vehicles

Tired of the same old Starfighters and speeders when you play mini-games? The Vehicles section of the Store has all the choices you'll ever need.

Under **Speeders**, you can find the fastest and flashiest speeder bikes in the Outer Rim! Collect them all, or pick a favorite like the flame-painted Zephyr-G speeder.

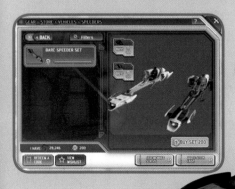

Under **Ships**, the best Starfighters in the fleet are ready for action! Choose from slick Jedi Starfighters or tough Y-wing bombers in all kinds of colors.

Using Your Vehicles in Games

Some games, like Speederbike Racing and Starfighter, let you select a personal vehicle from your collection just after the starting game screen.

Actions

You've got a lot of personality, so why not show it off? The Actions section of the Store lets you cut loose with some hot moves and even gives you a way to disguise yourself as somebody else!

Moves: Weapon moves packs, like the one designed to be used with the Republic flamethrower, let everyone know you mean business!

Holoprojectors: Want to step into someone else's shoes? These devices let you wear a temporary holographic disguise. Be a droideka, an Ithorian, or even a Gungan!

Mind Tricks: These special moves let you do flashy stunts like Force-glow or Force-push. The Republic cruiser mind trick makes a small fleet of ships orbit around your head!

All actions are available for use under your Actions menu once purchased.

Card Commander

The Store is a great place to sharpen your Card Commander gear. From the main Store menu, click Card Commander to review the booster packs and Holocrons  available for purchase. You can also get special rewards by winning campaigns and redeeming card codes.

Redeem a Code

Here you can see special items redeemable when you get Station Cash cards or redeem codes from stores. Special gifts to users from *Clone Wars*  *Adventures* are shown under the Bonus Items listing, like the golden mouse Droid that all players received when the game reached one million registered users!

Station Cash

What is Station Cash? This virtual money is used to buy premium items in *Clone Wars Adventures*. As soon as you add Station Cash to your in-game balance you can shop for items marked with a yellow Station Cash icon in the Store.

To purchase Station Cash, click the Add Station Cash button at the bottom of the Gear menu. You can also buy Station Cash on the *Clone Wars Adventures* website.

Certain stores offer Station Cash cards. These ten-dollar cards are worth one thousand Station Cash, and they also grant you a piece of armor from an exclusive set upon redemption online at clonewarsadventures.com!*

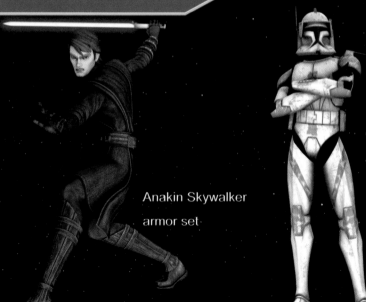

Commander Cody armor set

Anakin Skywalker armor set

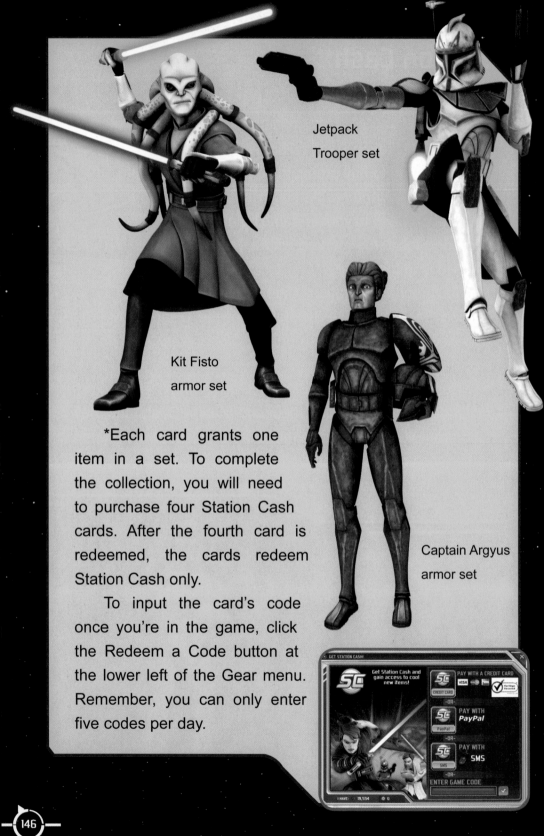

Jetpack
Trooper set

Kit Fisto
armor set

Captain Argyus
armor set

*Each card grants one item in a set. To complete the collection, you will need to purchase four Station Cash cards. After the fourth card is redeemed, the cards redeem Station Cash only.

To input the card's code once you're in the game, click the Redeem a Code button at the lower left of the Gear menu. Remember, you can only enter five codes per day.

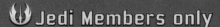

Jedi Members only

Once you're a Jedi Member, you'll find that many exclusive items in the Store are now available to you.

Browse the Jedi outfits worn by some of the great Jedi Masters from Shaak Ti to Obi-Wan Kenobi.

Is the life of a freelancer more your speed? Try out the gear worn by Aurra Sing or the unique hat of bounty hunter Embo.

Sometimes you just want to take a walk on the dark side! Jedi Members can outfit themselves to look like Asajj Ventress or put on the mad scientist garb of Separatist villain Nuvo Vindi.

Most of these outfits require Republic credits, so play lots of mini-games!

Item Sets

Really love that Mandalorian armor? Think your house isn't complete without the total Gungan look? Want to snap up some limited-edition seasonal items before they're gone? Item Sets are easy ways to get every piece of a set with a single click.

In the Store you can browse for gear, furnishings, actions, and more by set. Clicking on the set will let you study each individual item, but you can click Buy Set at the lower right to purchase everything at once. When you do, the bar under the set's name will fill up and you'll get a "Set Complete" message.

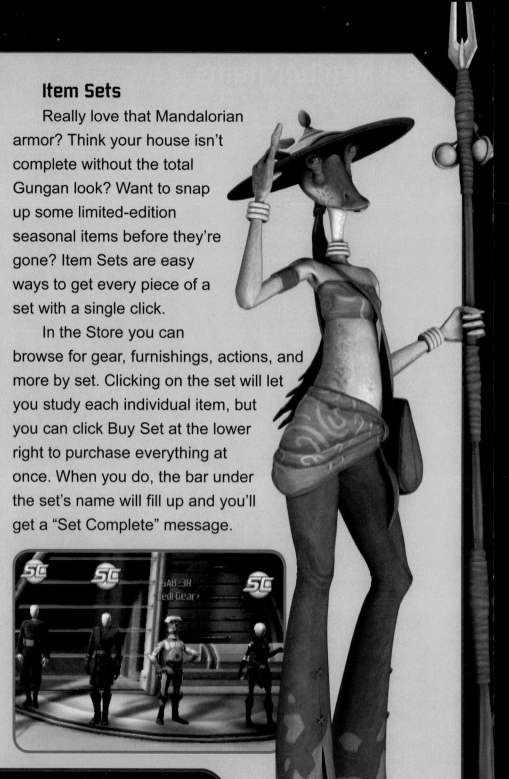

Gifting Items

Make a friend's day by giving the gift of cool gear, a friendly Droid, an awesome house decoration, or a limited-edition item!

Under your My Gear menu, click the Store button and browse for something your friend might like. Place your cursor over the item's icon, then select the Buy for Friend button to the right of the item. Not all items are available for gifting!

Next you'll see the Send a Gift menu, with a list of your friends on the left. Just click the lucky friend, click Purchase, and you're done! Your friend can accept the item under his or her Communications window. However, Station Cash items are not available for gifting.

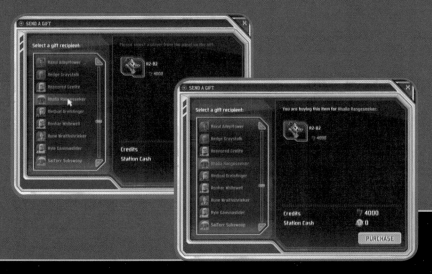

Your Wish List

It can be tough looking at the latest and coolest items in the Store if you don't have the credits to buy them yet! Don't worry—your wish list is an easy way to bookmark your favorite pieces of gear for later reference. Just place your cursor over the item you want to save, then click Wish List Add. Call up your wish list by clicking View Wish List at the bottom of the Gear menu.

Remember, other people can view your wish list. You can view theirs, too, by clicking the Gear tab on their profile.

Want to gift an item to another player? View their wish list to get ideas!

Don't wait too long! Some items are only available for a limited time.

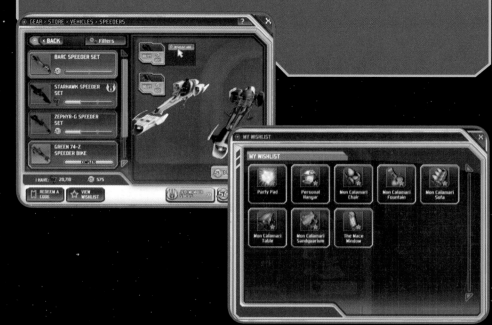

Help with Purchases

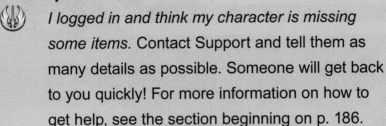

I logged in and think my character is missing some items. Contact Support and tell them as many details as possible. Someone will get back to you quickly! For more information on how to get help, see the section beginning on p. 186.

Will I lose my stuff if I cancel my Jedi Membership? No! Some items might not be available for play when you're not a Member, but everything will be waiting for you if you decide to renew.

Can I trade my purchases to another player? No, but you can buy items for another player as gifts.

Where are my new items? Check the Communicator window by clicking the envelope icon at the lower left. You might have a message asking you to accept a new item. Once you do, check My Gear to see your new stuff.

>> You get a Padawan Dormitory when you create your character. Jedi Members receive Jedi Living Quarters as an additional house, and you can even buy your own Attack Cruiser and hang out on its bridge! These are your homes, so visit whenever you need a break from the crowds or want to hang out with a small group of friends. Just click the My House button on the bottom right of the screen!

Once you're in your house, you'll see a new group of icons on the right side of the screen. These let you lock or unlock your house, return to the Temple, or open the Edit tool. To visit someone else's house, open the player's profile and click the Visit House button.

You can buy furniture for your house—and even special houses, like the Attack Cruiser—by checking out the Housing section of the Store.

Decorating Your House

Bring up the Edit menu by clicking the hammer-and-wrench icon on the right.

On the new menu, you'll see tabs that show furniture items by set.

🔵 Click one, and you'll see that you can now use your mouse to place the item anywhere in your house. Click your left mouse button to let go of the item.

🔵 Don't like the way it's facing? Click the item to bring up positioning controls. You can now rotate it to the right or left, or click the Move arrows to relocate it to a new spot.

🔵 Click the red slash circle if you want to pick up the item and return it to your inventory.

Visit your Trophy Room to admire the trophies you've earned in mini-games and to study the ones you want to get next!

Top Jedi Hangouts

Want to entertain your friends in a supercool party pad? Browse the Housing section of the Store to stock up on furnishings that reflect your personal style!

Do you love the water? Show off your aquatic side with the Mon Calamari set, which is a personal favorite of Admiral Ackbar!

No room is complete without a Mace Window! This stained-glass depiction of the famous Jedi Master will brighten up your wall.

Ranulph Archtracer

DROID DESTRUCTION
CHAMBER

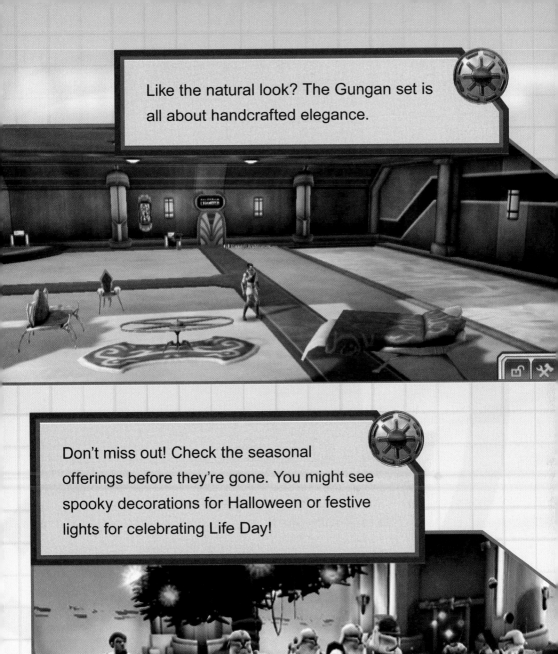

Like the natural look? The Gungan set is all about handcrafted elegance.

Don't miss out! Check the seasonal offerings before they're gone. You might see spooky decorations for Halloween or festive lights for celebrating Life Day!

Housing Modules

Jedi Members only

Jedi Members automatically get the Jedi Living Quarters as their second house. This huge apartment has giant windows, high ceilings, and even an indoor pool! Even better, Jedi Members can add additional rooms to their Jedi Living Quarters by shopping for Modules under the Housing section of the Store.

Party Pad: The perfect spot to host a crazy gathering for your friends! This exterior deck offers a great view of the Coruscant skyline.

Hidden Armory: Certain weapons by default will appear in your armory. It's not called "hidden" for nothing! To enter the armory, click the circular floor pad in the center of your house.

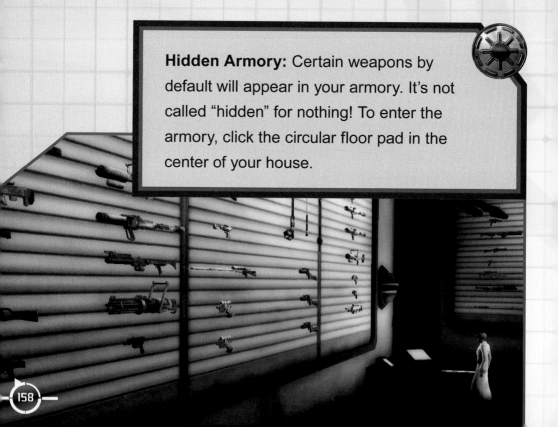

Droid Destruction Room: Smash some clankers! This testing chamber lets you unleash mines, grenades, blasters, and deactivator zappers against a regenerating squad of battle Droids. For more fun, run all four tests at once!

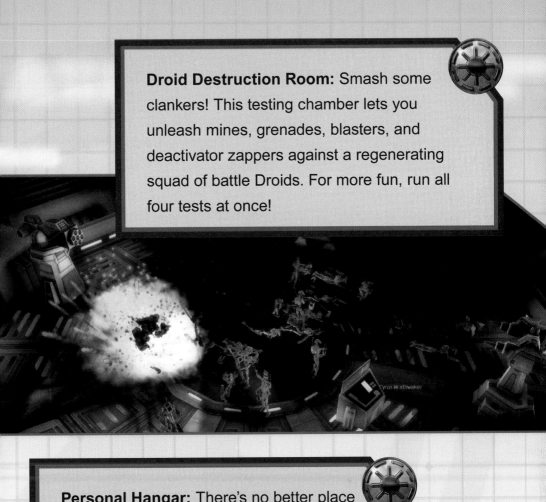

Personal Hangar: There's no better place to show off the starships and speeders you've collected than in your own hangar bay. Come visit them anytime—that is when you're not busy racing them in mini-games!

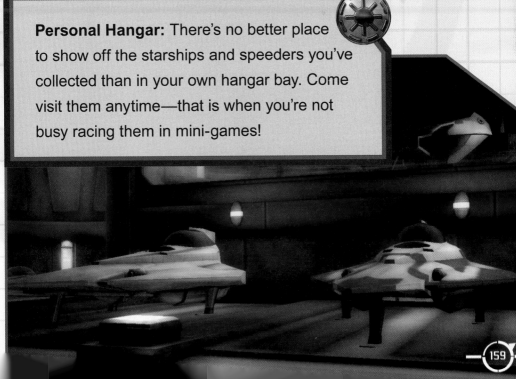

Attack Cruiser

The Attack Cruiser is a separate house that can be purchased using your Station Cash. Just go to the Housing section of the Store, then click Houses. To decide if you like the Attack Cruiser house before you buy it, click the Preview button after placing your cursor above the icon. You'll find yourself inside a full-scale copy!

The Attack Cruiser is a premium item that becomes an all-new house in addition to your Padawan Dormitory and, if you're a Jedi Member, your Jedi Living Quarters. It's a huge space that's perfect for welcoming lots of friends. Spend some time looking around and you'll notice lots of little details like the gaming alcove, the map of the *Star Wars*® galaxy, and the interactive control panel at the front of the bridge. Click it to trigger some fun effects!

Red alert: Emergency! Clicking this button will start up the sirens and turn on a flashing red light indicating a Separatist attack is near!

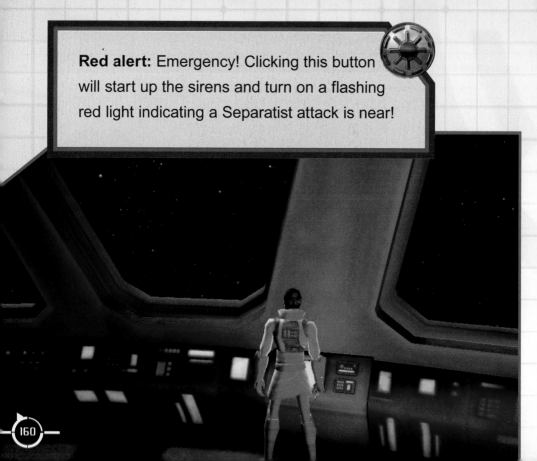

Launch fighters: Choose this to order a squadron of Y-wings to zoom out of your hangar bay. You can view them through the bridge windows as they patrol for danger.

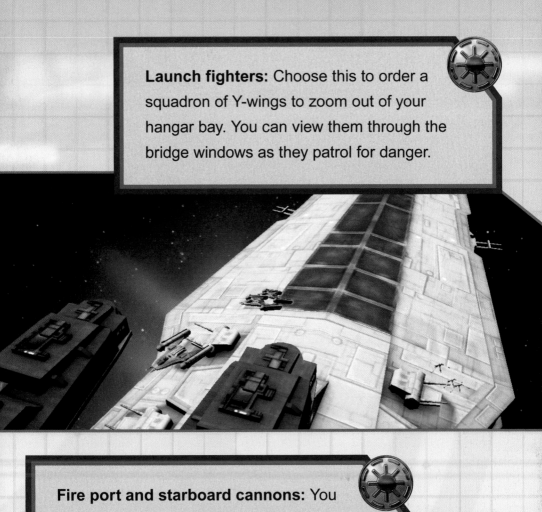

Fire port and starboard cannons: You have the power! Order your gunners to fire the turbolaser batteries on either side of your ship and hear the roar of heavy weapons!

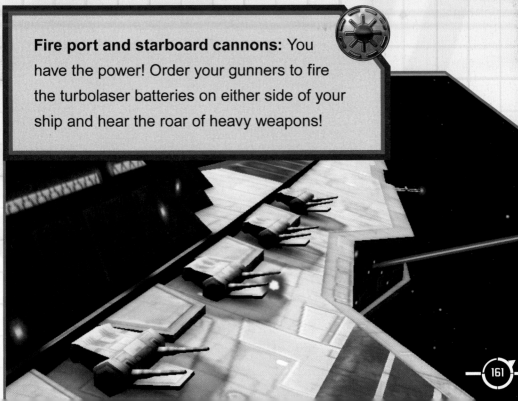

My Gear

The My Gear menu is a great place to manage armor, weapons, and all your other stuff! On the left-hand side of the menu you'll see shortcuts to your collections of headgear, clothing, gloves, shoes, weapons, furniture, Droid parts, creature gear, vehicles, and actions. Clicking any of these

shows what you own in that category. What you're wearing right now will show up as the last item, highlighted in green. Move your mouse over any item and click Equip to wear it!

 To see everything you're wearing in one place, click Equipped Gear at the very top of the list.

 Under any category, you can click the Get More button at the lower right to jump directly to the Store!

Shopping for Outfits

Under the Store menu, choose Outfits. Here you'll see lots of categories including Clone Trooper Gear, Jedi Gear, Bounty Hunter Gear, and more. Choose the set you want to browse, and the pieces in that set will appear at the right. You'll see the price and whether it requires Republic credits or Station Cash.

 Click an item to buy it, preview it on your character before you buy it, or add it to your wish list to buy later.

 Some item sets are only available for Jedi Members. These are marked with the winged Lightsaber Jedi Member icon.

What's Your Look?

You can wear any item by clicking Equip after placing your cursor above the item's icon. But you don't need to wear every item in a set! Find your own look by mixing and matching pieces from different outfits. What about bounty hunter armor mashed up with a Lightsaber and the boots worn by the Mandalorian secret service?

 Want people to see your face? Wear your Clone Trooper armor, but unequip the helmet.

 You can try a different outfit every time you log in!

 Some outfits are available for only a limited time, like the Spiked Trooper armor from Halloween or the Republic Nutcracker outfit from Life Day!

Cool Looks

New outfits are added to the Store all the time. Here are a few of the coolest and funniest sets that have appeared since the game's launch.

Zillo Beast Costume:
Only available during Halloween, this set turned you into a big, green lizard!

Ahsoka Tano:
Ahsoka's new look is perfectly reproduced in this sleek set.

Flamethrower Clone Trooper:
You can take the heat in this heavily armored outfit, and dish it out, too, with a two-handed flamethrower.

Cad Bane:
Twin blaster pistols and that unforgettable hat make this outfit the highlight of the bounty hunter gear sets!

Wampa Suit:
This Jedi Member exclusive costume is white and fluffy, but hopefully not too itchy!

≫ *Star Wars®* just wouldn't be the same without Droids or Creatures. Some are bad news, like the Separatists' battle Droids. But most are loyal, friendly, and will do anything to help their masters.

In *Clone Wars Adventures*, Droids and Creatures are Pets that you can collect and then display to other players whenever you want. Call a Pet by clicking the Pets icon on the left-hand side of the screen. This brings up a list of all your Pets. Pick the one you want and it'll stay by your side! Call up the same menu

MY PETS! (4)
1M-AU5 5T-U85
RA-7 TO-DO
BUY NOW!

to send your Pet away or to bring out a different Pet.

Pets can be purchased from the Store and are sometimes given out to all players for special occasions. The Astromech B3-T4 was given to all players who participated in the early beta testing for *Clone Wars Adventures*!

Not sure what Pet is right for you? Browse through the Store for the latest models that have been shipped to Coruscant. Most Pets fit into the following categories:

Protocol Droids: C-3PO is an excellent protocol Droid, even if he is a little jumpy! Protocol Droids are shaped like humans and are excellent translators.

Astromech Droids: Like R2-D2, these short, wheeled Droids are great at fixing things. They are fearless and will never abandon you!

Mouse Droids: These little guys love to zip around. Watch your step if there's a mouse Droid in the room!

Power Droids: These walking batteries don't have much personality, but who can resist their call of "gonk, gonk"?

Other Droids: Keep your eyes open and you might see Cad Bane's techno-service Droid, Todo, or even a miniature AT-AT walker in Droid form!

Tricked-Out Pet Gear

Want to give your Pet some extra bling? Click the gear-shaped icon next to the Pet icon. This lets you equip a special part or remove an already equipped part. The Store has lots of options for customizing your Pet, and here are a few favorites:

Astromech blastromech gear: Turn your astromech into a mobile blaster turret with this hazardous upgrade.

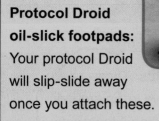

Protocol Droid oil-slick footpads: Your protocol Droid will slip-slide away once you attach these.

Techno-Service Droid explosive device: Stand back! With this add-on, Todo goes boom!

Seasonal gear: Some of the best gear is only available during special occasions. During Halloween, protocol Droids could get a General Grievous costume. During December's Life Day festivities, astromechs could obtain a snow maker and mouse Droids could get a windup key!

BO-LT5: This astromech has teeth painted on his dome, and his three visual sensors make him look like a monster. But he's friendly, honest!

J3-3V3: You never know when this protocol Droid might get you out of a diplomatic jam.

SP-OT: What's better than an AT-AT as a Pet? An AT-AT that walks on two legs! Be sure to add the bipedal datacard to SP-OT.

5T-U85: He might not look like much, but this power Droid has got it where it counts! Upgrade him with Droid parts from the Store.

>> *Clone Wars Adventures* is a great place to chat, socialize, and have fun! One of the best things about the game is the opportunity to meet new people. When you're not busy shopping or playing mini-games, you can hang out in the Main Hall or in any of the other rooms of the Jedi Temple. If you see a player you want to add as a friend, click the player's character and then click the Add as Friend button to send a friend request.

Other players might add you as a friend, too! You'll see a notice pop up on your screen when this happens. You have the choice to accept or reject the friend request. If you miss the pop-up window, the friend request will be saved in your Communicator messages.

Ranulph Archtracer

Your Buddy List

The Buddy List is a handy shortcut for checking to see which of your friends are online and to quickly interact with any friend you choose.

Click the Friends button at lower left to bring up your Buddy List. At top you'll see the number of friends you have in total, and a list of pictures and names underneath. Friends currently online will appear at the top of the list with their names in white. The names of offline friends are listed in gray.

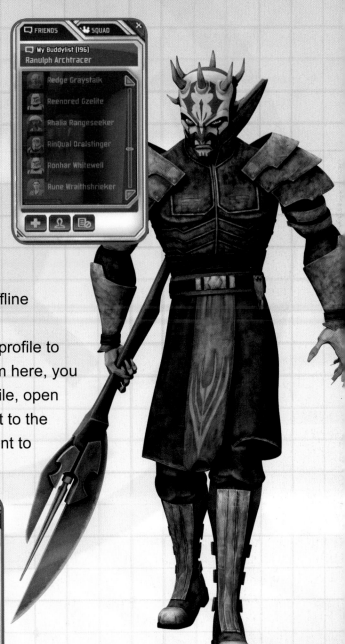

Click on any friend's profile to call up a mini-menu. From here, you can view the friend's profile, open a chat window, or teleport to the friend's location if you want to hang out in person.

View Profile: Call up a friend's profile to remind yourself of their favorite things or to compare their gaming trophies to yours!

Chat: Open a special chat window between only you and your friend.

Teleport to Friend: Click this to jump instantly to wherever your friend is right now.

Invite Player to Squad: Are you recruiting new squad members or starting a new squad from scratch? Click on this to invite the currently selected friend to join your group.

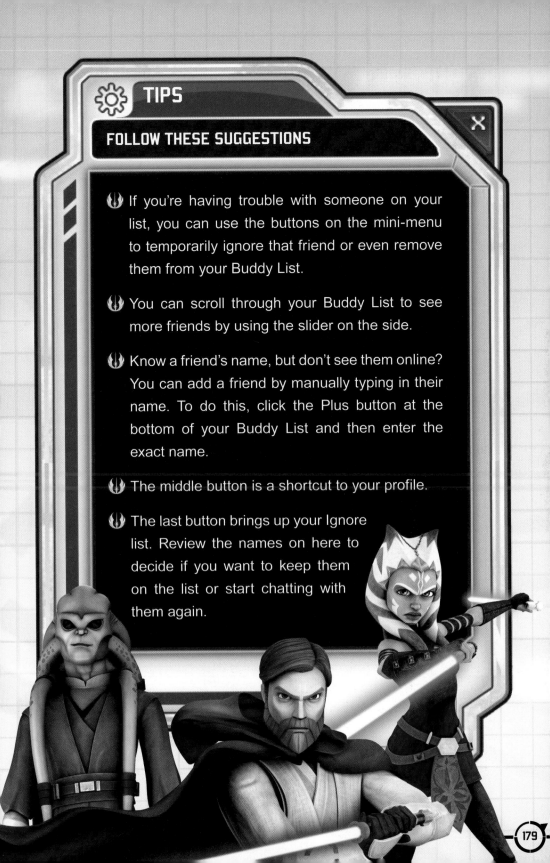

⚙ TIPS

FOLLOW THESE SUGGESTIONS

If you're having trouble with someone on your list, you can use the buttons on the mini-menu to temporarily ignore that friend or even remove them from your Buddy List.

You can scroll through your Buddy List to see more friends by using the slider on the side.

Know a friend's name, but don't see them online? You can add a friend by manually typing in their name. To do this, click the Plus button at the bottom of your Buddy List and then enter the exact name.

The middle button is a shortcut to your profile.

The last button brings up your Ignore list. Review the names on here to decide if you want to keep them on the list or start chatting with them again.

Squads

With a squad, you and your friends can hang out together and chat on a private channel. Squads are also a great way to meet new friends among the ranks of your squadmates.

Jedi Members can access the Squads tab on the Buddy List. When creating a squad for the first time, type in the squad name you'd like to use,

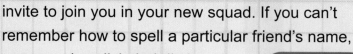

and submit it for a moderator's okay. Once it's approved, click the + button at the bottom of the Squads tab, and type in the name of any player you want to invite to join you in your new squad. If you can't remember how to spell a particular friend's name, you can also click their listing on your Buddy List. Then select "Invite Player to Squad."

As a squad leader, you have the ability to promote members to different ranks and to set the squad's welcome message on the Squads tab. Remember, your squad can use its own private chat channel!

Chatting

Chatting with your friends and other players is what makes *Clone Wars Adventures* a fun place to socialize! To chat with a friend, click the character and then Send Message or click your friend's name in your Buddy List. Type what you want to say in the chat field and hit Enter or click Send to talk. You can minimize this window to get it out of your way by clicking the button at the top right.

To chat with other people around you, type in the chat bar at the bottom center of the screen. The globe icon to the left of the bar brings up the World Chat log where you can read your comments and those of everybody around you!

Challenging Your Friends!

The mini-games in *Clone Wars Adventures* are a blast, but they pack even more power when you play with friends! Several games allow you to invite friends from your Buddy List for multiplayer matches.

Click Invite Friends on the game's starting screen and you'll see all your online friends. Click their names to invite them to play!

Speederbike Racing: Choose a stage and choose up to three friends for full-throttle action!

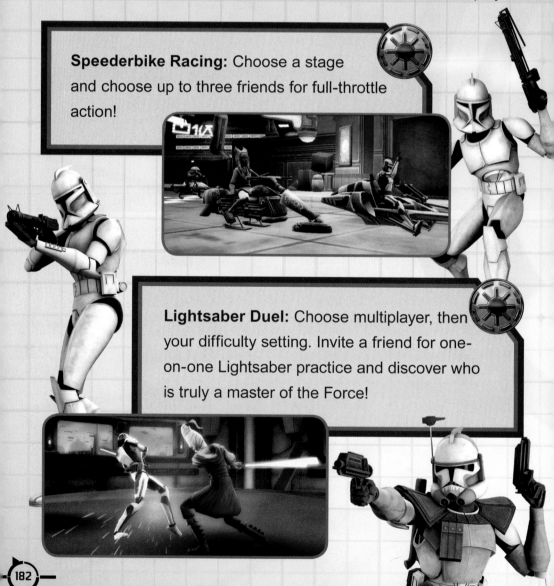

Lightsaber Duel: Choose multiplayer, then your difficulty setting. Invite a friend for one-on-one Lightsaber practice and discover who is truly a master of the Force!

Multiplayer Challenge Menu

When you click on a fellow player in-game, a radial menu that gives you a selection of games that you can play with that person will pop up. (More games will be available if you and the other person are both Jedi Members.) Click one of the game icons to challenge the player or click the red X at the center to get rid of the multiplayer menu.

Member Events

Looking for more ways to get to know other players? Attend one of the regular member events held in-game! These fun, casual gatherings happen at a certain time and meeting place, like the Main Hall or the Hangar.

- Times and places for member events are listed on the main *Clone Wars Adventures* website under the Latest News section.

- Member events are hosted by members of the official Community Team. All of them have the title Emissary in front of their names.

- Want to jump right to the party? Add Emissary Event to your Buddy List. (See p. 179 for more information on manually adding friends.) When the event comes online in your Buddy List, click the listing and click Teleport.

Taking Screen Shots

Sometimes the best memories are captured in photos. *Clone Wars Adventures* takes place through your computer, but that doesn't mean you can't make and save your own snapshots!

Press the F12 key to take a screen shot of the current game screen. You can then find the picture under the Sony Online Entertainment folder on your hard drive, under the ImageCaptureOutput subfolder. Go to help.clonewarsadventures.com for more detailed instructions if you have trouble.

Screen shots are great ways to remember a jaw-dropping costume, a rocking member event, or the incredible way you've decorated your house!

>> Remember, getting help in the game is as easy as a single click. If you're having a problem for any reason, click the question mark Help icon at the top right of your screen.

If you've spotted something in the game that isn't working like it should, click Report a Bug. Describe the problem in as much detail as you can in the window, then click Submit.

If you're having trouble with other players, have a question, or aren't sure where your problem should go, click Ask for Help. This will take you to the Support website at help.clonewarsadventures.com where you can contact a Counselor.

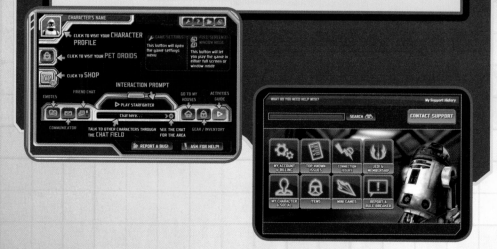

Counselors

Counselors are official staff members of *Clone Wars Adventures* and are here to help! If you're playing the game, you might see one of our Counselors hanging out in the Main Hall or near one of the gaming stations. Don't be afraid to say hi!

A Counselor can also come to your aid if you're having trouble with other players, need more information about the game, or even if you are stuck behind an obstacle. If you don't see a Counselor in the game world, contact Support by clicking the question mark Help button at the upper right and clicking Ask for Help.

Enforcers: These members of the Enforcement Department mean business! Enforcers protect players from rule breakers by issuing suspensions and bans.

Online Help

Sometimes you might need help when you're not playing, or maybe you need help logging in. There are lots of ways to get help outside the game.

 For general questions, go directly to the support site at help.clonewarsadventures.com. Here, you can browse by category or search for a particular keyword.

 Still stuck? You can contact a Counselor outside the game by clicking the green Contact Support button at the bottom of any article on the support site. Someone will answer as soon as they can!

 You can also contact technical support over the phone at 858-537-0898. This is not a toll-free call, so be sure to get your parents' permission before calling.

For Parents

Parents wanting to know more about their children's experience in *Clone Wars Adventures* are encouraged to take an active role. An overview of the basics of the game can be found online at clonewarsadventures.com/forParents.html. Here you'll find information on parental controls, how to set up your child's account, how to set limits on game play, and the steps that *Clone Wars Adventures* takes to ensure your child's privacy.

Many problems with technical issues or billing, from getting the game to launch to adding Station Cash with a credit card, are covered in detail in the searchable archive at help.clonewarsadventures.com.